Published in Great Britain by
L.R. Price Publications Ltd, 2023

27 Old Gloucester Street,
London, WC1N 3AX
www.lrpricepublications.com

Cover artwork by
L.R. Price Publications Ltd

ISBN: 978-1-916613-16-4

Rachel Finds Herself as Lydia Plays

S.M. Stephens

Arriving

Josh Goldstein arrived at a murky, overcast Manchester Piccadilly. He was on the 1:00 p.m. train from London Euston to meet his new family in a middle-class suburb of Manchester. Prestwich is one of those places that you may spot on a city map, but when arriving are disappointed to realise it has little soul, except for its mainly Edwardian type homes or modern, tall, boring, glass apartments - all looking exactly the same.

Josh checked his Chinese-made Rolex and realised he had twenty minutes to kill before the arrival of his ride to meet the relatives. He met them once on the day he took his wedding vows; that was three years ago, when he married his one and only Jewish girlfriend, Rachel. At the time, he thought this to be a smart idea; it would keep his own family happy, and he would be able to carry on as before with his harem of gentile mistresses. Jewish girls were for appearances, respectability, stability - and above all, business contacts. Other girls were for blowjobs, nightclubs, and for show when you required a blonde-haired trophy on your arm. The main drawback with Jewish girls was one of passion: if you grabbed their hair, it would slip off and destroy the moment. You see, such religious girls insisted on covering up at all times; this included hiding themselves under the duvet in darkness. Thankfully, his Rachel was not quite like that.

His thoughts were broken by a friendly "beep-beep". A tatty, light blue 2009 Volvo screeched to a halt along the station concourse, prompting angry blasts of less amicable horns; Manchester's Finest, its black taxi trade, was not happy - they hated anyone else near what they considered their station. In their eyes, this was their turf, no one else's.

The driver of Sweden's finest tank waved at him and said, "Josh, jump in." Josh obliged and shook the stubby hand that was offered to him. He noticed the index finger was missing and all that remained was a short stump.

"I'm Daniel, but my friends and enemies call me 'Stumpy.'" Josh nodded and hopped into the front passenger seat of the car. For the moment he kept silent and observed the car's well-worn surroundings, unsure who or what was more worn. His new companion was at least twenty-five years his senior. Stumpy was dressed completely in black, complete with a tatty black fabric hat, but most striking were the full, grey beard and thick neck. The car itself smelled of stale Salmon and Marlboro cigarettes, the windscreen covered in a thin film of tobacco residue. The engine tappets sounded as worn as the interior looked. Stumpy pulled away abruptly from the yelling black taxi drivers. Josh used the opportunity to shut his eyes and thought of his brunette paramour in London.

The conversation on the journey to his relatives (not new, but unseen since his wedding day) was strained to say the least. He was not sure what he thought of Stumpy; for one he was clearly a typical Northerner. Josh came to this conclusion after Stumpy lit his third cigarette of the journey without offering the pack. This reminded Josh why he kept his distance from people north of the Watford Gap.

Josh helped himself to the packet, lit a smoke with the car lighter, inhaled, and exhaled, watching the smoke collect on the windscreen adding to the car's tarnished interior.

Stumpy grinning said, "I shot the last person that took something off me; you're not an Arsenal supporter, are you?"

"No," Josh replied, "I'm a Yiddo," and they both laughed. This broke the ice.

Josh was quietly surprised about his companion; he decided they had a lot in common, but something bothered him. Stumpy's appearance and demeanour did not seem to mix with the conversation they were having. Two more Marlboro's later, the Volvo pulled on to a gravel drive and parked beside another Volvo: a shiny new five-door hatch-back. Josh similarly noted the silver sports Mercedes and British racing green Mini Cooper S.

Before Stumpy switched off the clanking engine, the front door opened, and a stream of children ran out of the open front door. They were of different ages, from what looked like four to ten, but strangely only boys, all wearing the same scruffy style suits that Stumpy wore except smaller. The youngest boys' clothes were the most worn, clearly hand-me-downs, their heads covered with a kippah, the headgear of religious Jewish people. "What a waste," thought Josh, "I'll have to do some converting".

Before he could think further, an old man appeared, inviting Josh in with a slight hint of a Polish accent. As he entered the home, Josh observed Stumpy cutting open his Volvo's spare tyre with what appeared to be an old-fashioned blade. Josh could see its distinct ivory handle reflect off the only shiny bit of the car.

The old man shut the front door loudly and beckoned Josh in.

"I'm Max," he said, "Rachel's Grandfather. I'm sorry we have not met before, but I was away at the time of your wedding - an unfortunate last-minute business trip."

"I understand, as I remember Rachel explained the

situation to me."

Josh followed Max down the dark hallway. He noticed how familiar Max was. He reminded him of Rachel; Josh shuddered at the thought of her as an old woman. It was not a pretty sight. The pair entered the second door on the right, leading into a large dark wood furnished living room.

"Charming to meet you. I'm Rachel's Bubbe," an elderly lady said, her Polish accent not as pronounced as Max. "Josh, I'm Sofia."

Josh shook her warm outstretched hand.

"Rachel's told me all about you, your wedding photo stands above our fireplace. You were a handsome couple - well, you still are."

"What a charmer, already. My Rachel warned me of your silver tongue, now stop flattering an old lady and meet the family."

Sofia flapped her arms and an array of Jewish men appeared from the door facing Josh. He was surprised for a second; he was not expecting an all-male party. Everyone took a seat, the oldest on the most uncomfortable looking high-backed wooden chair which reminded Josh of Jewish mourning chairs. They were uncomfortable and unforgiving, as they should be on sad occasions; it was as if the old men were deliberately testing the younger generation to see how much mourning they could manage. However, the strongest and the youngest slouched down on the more comfortable pair of three-seater leather sofas. Josh guessed whatever the elderly men had planned backfired, as the younger guys got to the comfortable seats first. He was introduced to them all by Max. Sofia was the only woman there. She was Max's wife and she made it clear this was her domain, the matriarch of the family home. Josh knew he would not remember the names, but he tried to make a mental note. David, Simon, Gary, and Mark, with David being the youngest and Mark the oldest of the grandchildren. They were all thickset and dressed in typical religious clothing, like Max, but their clothing was of a finer and more modern quality. He also noted that they all wore wedding rings except Simon. He was the only one not wearing traditional clothing; in fact, he looked rather flamboyant.

"A drink?" offered Max.

"Gary-whisky all round please. Will Jameson's do?"

Max looked directly at Josh as he spoke in a typical Eastern European tone.

Josh nodded and accepted a smoke from Mark - a thick Cuban cigar. Things were looking up, thought Josh.

The cigar, to Josh's surprise, was exceedingly fresh, probably a Bolivar, from the esteemed company in Havana known as Rocha and Co., originally a product of South America.

His thoughts were interrupted by a female voice from the facing door.

"Dinner is served."

Max was first to rise from his uncomfortable seat, having difficulty doing so alone, but David was quick on his toes and assisted his grandfather. Max beckoned Sofia to join him. The others meekly followed as if following orders. Josh took his cue and did likewise.

Gary drew back the old-fashioned sliding doors to a large connecting dining room, nearly double the size of the main living room. Max sat at the head of the table as the others followed and sat at what Josh would guess was their regular eating places. He noted empty seats next to each of the men, except Simon. The reason for this was soon clear to him. Three women entered the room and took their seats next to their husbands, again as if on cue.

Sofia, sitting opposite Max, introduced each of the wives. First was David's wife, Sara, dressed in plain dark clothing: a long black skirt, grey blouse buttoned up to her neck, and a black wig - a sign of a religious nut, thought Josh. Next up was Gary's wife, Eve. She was wearing similar clothing, except that her long skirt was black and the blouse white, but tight fitting. Josh could see that Eve had a fine figure, or at least a pert pair of rounded breasts. They looked like they wanted to jump out and play. Josh smiled and shied away to try to distract himself from such thoughts; after all, they were family. He noted the framed portraits of elderly-looking Rabbis and pictures of

Jerusalem hanging from the walls. Pride of place was a family portrait in front of the Wailing Wall, with Rachel smiling and dressed attractively, staring back at him. The wall behind was covered in 1970s style sparkle plain textured wallpaper. The last introduced was Mark's wife. She again was dressed the same as the other two, but unlike the others was at least twenty stone. This was not a problem as Mark was the same size. In fact, in Josh's eyes he looked like a penguin. From now on that would be Mark's name, at least in Josh's own mind. She was Alison.

Formalities over, conversations sprung up from all sides of the table. Josh tried to listen in to the various chats, but realised this was useless as the family was speaking in Yiddish, or as Josh liked to say "Rubbish".

Gary realised Josh looked bemused and said, "English only please - he is our guest or should I say, family."

All eyes focused on Max. He raised a hand and said, "Gary is correct, be polite, he – Josh," pointing firmly, "is family and I want him treated as such."

Max called in Stumpy, who was in the garden playing with the kids.

"Stumpy, you will eat with us today. After all, you're family too."

Max gave Sofia a look, and she immediately clapped her hands and an array of waiting staff entered the room: all female, wearing below-knee black skirts and white buttoned blouses, all carrying bowls of chicken soup. Josh clocked the prominent name on the servers' badge reading simply "Pepper Wilder."

What did it mean, he wondered?

He also noticed the most attractive waitress, a Caribbean girl with a stunning afro, giving him the eye. Josh in his usual way gave her a look that said it all. After all, he was an East End lad. What is it they say? "You can't take the East End out of the Boy".

The main course was, naturally, roast chicken with roast potatoes with a gravy sauce, following the starter of chicken soup which Josh had never enjoyed before. He was not sure if it was to his taste. The Caribbean girl certainly was! Simon had caught sight of this, but except for a sly wink, said nothing. This was, after all, a Jewish dinner table.

After dessert came after-dinner prayers lead by Max, with David indicating to Josh when he should say "amen".

Noting that the wives only engaged in conversation after prayers, except mild chit-chat during dinner, Sofia stiffly rose from the table and left the room followed politely by the wives. The only lady remaining was the stunning waitress, as the others did not return after clearing the dinner table.

"Coffee and cigars" she said in Mancunian accent.

This surprised Josh, he was not expecting such a

sexy, husky voice.

"To business," said Max as Sofia left, after kissing Max gently on his cheek. The other men cut and lit their own cigars, but to Josh's surprise, the waitress – Lydia - cut his in courtesy. She handled the cigar in a somewhat provocative sexual nature, which Josh decided was for his benefit. He tried to precipitate this as he deeply inhaled the cigar, trying to get it to burn correctly and to keep her attention. He did not want her to think he was some kind of uncouth East-Ender. Thankfully as with all good cigars, the job was easy. She left him with the cheap lighter, which he noticed had an embossed emblem of a wildebeest and a pepper pot with the words Pepper Wilder, the same as the badge on her too tight-fitting black uniform, which did a perfect job of accentuating her curvaceous form. He also pocketed the blue notepaper, which she slyly handed him.

Max, noticing the flirtatious activity, said, "Josh since you are so interested in the contents of that uniform, I suggest we start there already."

Josh felt his face redden, aware all eyes were on him. He did the only thing he could think of: he squeezed Lydia's perfect arse, grinning, and retorted, "When you're ready, Max."

"Gentleman now Josh has had his fun, let's begin. Mark, you start and don't hold back; Josh is family and as such should know our business. As of today, what is ours is his."

Josh just sat there looking dumbfounded, not sure what to expect or to where this was leading. Mark struggled as he raised himself from his chair and took his place beside Max. He attempted to puff out his chest in an attempt to establish an air of importance but failed miserably, as all that puffed out was his stomach and the smoke from his cigar. Mark had his problems, most noticeably his weight, diabetes, and worst of all, his wife Alison. She was a nagger of the first order. In his mind she had created his health problems entirely, without ever a moment's peace, especially when at home in their large house situated in one of those expensive gated developments off the Middleton Road. It was always nag, nag, nag, but at least she gave him space - probably too much. In his younger days, he certainly took full advantage.

Max coughed and Mark took his cue and began to outline the general business of the family. Josh stretched out on the uncomfortable chair and listened intently, whilst never taking his eyes off Lydia who was loitering in the corner close to the second door.

Pepper Wilder was a pole-dancing members only club, close to Manchester's main Piccadilly railway station. The family owned and ran it over the last couple of years after taking it as collateral on a large gambling debt - naturally, on a no return basis. Josh was somewhat surprised and pricked up his ears. He hoped his over-interest did not show. Things got even more interesting when the Penguin revealed that this was one of the family's main legal enterprises. Mark, it appeared, oversaw the smooth running of all business, legal and not so legal. In fact, he was Max's right-hand man - or trouble-shooter, as he preferred.

As with most dancing clubs, the family also had control over the girls out-of-hours activities and a couple of rundown massage parlours to boot. David managed the club and was the "go to" guy disgruntled customers' sought. Simon was the main man customers looked to for favours or a line of Charlie - cocaine, to give it is its correct name. One of the favours (and most profitable pro-rata) was to ask permission to use the family name when other Jewish families suffered problems but lacked the muscle or nous to deal with them, ranging from kosher food not been up to standard at a Bar mitzvah, or a gambling debt.

The penguin shuffled uncomfortably and struggled to stay on his feet. With Max's say-so, Lydia placed a chair behind him. Mark almost fell into it gratefully. Josh had now switched off, as the conversation changed to the day-to-day running of things. As it did not interest him in the slightest, he focused on Lydia's dark attentive eyes until Stumpy stood up, left the room, and returned a moment later with a bottle of kosher wine, loudly plonking it on the table. This jolted Josh back to attention, especially when Max stated, "And now, Josh, to you and what we offer our latest family member, and more importantly keeping my granddaughter happy."

At this juncture, Josh actually felt himself jump. He did not actually realise how bent or organised the family were. He was shady, but not to this extent. He merely dealt in a bit of "stolen" or "gems" as he called it and handled the odd small shipment of illegal drugs if it came his way. No wonder Rachel never questioned the large bundle of notes he frequently left on the kitchen table, nor ever requested receipts for jewellery he bought home for her, usually when feeling guilty after screwing his latest lover.

Max took over from the Penguin and began to outline Josh's role within the business, firstly by reaching across the table, picking up the kosher wine bottle and handing it to Josh.

"What do you notice? Have a good look. What is it you cockneys say? ''Av a butchers.'"

Josh, laughing, examined the bottle to no avail. He noted that it was full and had the "Kosher for Passover" seal.

"No idea mate," forgetting where he was.

Max laughed heartily, "I'll show you." After picking up a gavel concealed under his seat, he smashed the bottle. Red wine seeped across the dining room table, dripping over Josh's trouser leg. Josh appreciated it to be a deliberate act as Max sat there laughing incessantly, generating laughter from his grandchildren.

Lydia offered to dab his trousers dry, creating more laughter.

Max intervened and said, "Come on boys, behave."

Josh then noticed several red condoms. The Penguin indicated that he should pick one up. Josh did as suggested, and on opening the rubber realised that it contained a white powdery substance; he instinctively knew what it was and promptly rubbed some on his gums, produced an American Express card and cut some lines on a dry part of the table, loudly snorting it up both nostrils. Josh deliberately did not share, but exclaimed, "Bloody hell, this is grade A stuff!"

"Naturally, you can taste the quality already," Max said, "my late father brought me up that way. He always said if you supply quality, you will always have food on the table. He broke off, deep in thought. Josh swore he could see a tear on Max's face. He said nothing.

The penguin, realising that his grandfather was struggling, took over and began outlining the system, explaining eloquently Josh's involvement.

Josh turned the information over in his head, and after three long years realised that marrying Rachel could be his ticket to a regular income and real respectability. It appeared that he would be running the London arm of this operation.

Gary took an iPhone out of his jacket pocket and slid it across the table, saying "All you need is in there, and - it goes without saying - be careful with it."

Max turned his attention to Lydia, who was still loitering in the corner, and asked very politely if she could be so kind as to bring in the good whisky and a cloth to wipe clean the wine sodden table. She pulled a disgruntled face but did as requested. Table-wiping was not her remit; dancing on them, however, a different matter. She resurfaced within five minutes and Josh observed that she had applied fresh lipstick and a dab of Chanel, probably no 5. Lydia placed a bottle of Lagavulin on the table and began mopping the table slowly bending lower than needed, deliberately revealing her ample cleavage, Simon and Josh both noticing that she had undone two buttons on her shirt. Drinks now poured, Max rose from his seat and said, "A toast."

The table's occupants rose, in unison raising their glasses, except for the penguin who naturally struggled to get up - once up, they all drank in one gulp, staring at Josh as they swallowed. Josh raised his glass in similar fashion and cleared his crystal cut in a similar fashion, acknowledging the intent of the toast. More drinks were poured by Lydia, but this time drunk in a leisurely fashion. David produced a pack of cards.

"Poker gentlemen?"

Josh noticed the Pepper Wilder emblem on the pack: the wording was highlighted in gold, with a gold embossed shape of a wildebeest on a black background, and a shapely nude female figure astride the beast. David shuffled and dealt them round the table, smiling to himself for this was his game.

Lydia was told her day was done and left the room, it seemed to Josh rather abruptly. She did appear to be enjoying herself, especially since she had repositioned herself behind him.

A few hours later the bottle of scotch stood empty, with the lion's share of the folding in front of Josh. The game was down to two players: himself, and David. The room was now warmer and somewhat smoke-filled. Max, being a wise old man, had seen this many times before and stopped the battle of wits, which was intense between the two remaining players.

He said simply, "Josh, have you got the time?" Josh broke off from his serious concentration and looked at his Chinese Rolex.

"Ahem, it's-"

He broke off. The cheap copy had stopped at 6:00 p.m. He knew it had to be about midnight. On seeing this, David unstrapped his own watch and threw it across to him. Josh caught it and saw that it was a Rolex – the same as his, except by the feel of it, this one was real, and it said 1:20 a.m.

"I can't take this."

"You're not," David said, as he leaned over and helped himself to the folding. Josh was at a loss on how to react.

Max, being the instigator of this completely new game took total control, and said, "You wear it, you've bought it."

The laughter that followed showed Josh that he had lost. He retired to what he imagined was his best option and replied, "Lovely Kettle, 'fanks."

"That's alright, I've got three like it."

Unbeknownst to Josh, David had a gambling problem, and it was not the first time Max had bailed him out. Stumpy, who had hardly said a word all night, suggested that it had been a long day for Josh and that he would drive him to the family-connected hotel he was staying the night in. All agreed this was a sensible move. Hands were shaken all round. Josh, not forgetting his manners, asked Max to thank Sofia for her hard work and hospitality. Max, tired, grunted an acknowledgement.

Stumpy led Josh to the front door opened it. The fresh early-morning air hit them both as they breathed it deep into their smoke-filled lungs.

Meet & Greet...

The sound of a hotel room telephone ringing brought Josh out of his alcohol-induced sleep. At first, he thought the annoying sound was part of his dream; its persistence told him otherwise. His hand reached out to where the offending tone came from.

“’Ello,” he said groggily.

A husky female voice replied, “I’m in the lobby. How about lunch?”

His mind, still not yet awake, could not comprehend the voice nor recognise it, answering with an “Err...”

“It's Lydia; I’ll see you in the lobby in thirty minutes.” Josh grunted and hung up.

Eyes now open, he looked at his surroundings. The room was typical of a mid-price hotel; it contained all the usual items you would expect. He vaguely recalled Stumpy mentioning a tour of the family business premises and introduction of associates. The thought of Lydia downstairs spurred him out of bed. He found the shower, tripping up over his badly placed suitcase. Lovingly packed by Rachel, it contained enough clothing for fourteen days. She did this on instruction from her grandfather. Refreshed and now fully awake, dressed in a pair of Levi’s and a black buttoned casual shirt, Josh left his room and followed the signs to the lift.

On arrival at lobby level, he scanned his eyes for

Lydia. She was sitting on a comfortable leather sofa, partially blocked by a vase of fresh flowers. Josh ambled straight over, first glancing at his new Rolex - it said 12:30 p.m. - and then at Lydia. She smiled in acknowledgement. Lydia was also out of uniform - not literally, of course, but dressed in a business suit with a skirt that had a perfectly proportioned slit, showing just enough thigh as she sat demurely with her legs crossed.

"Afternoon. Long night, was it?" she said, grinning.

She already knew this, as Mark had called her and told her to put back the collection time. Josh winked as he took in her fine figure.

"Coffee first," he said.

His head was beginning to throb, reacting badly to last night's whisky. He tried to hide this, but again she knew.

"Why not?" was the reply.

The pair walked over to the hotel breakfast restaurant. Josh glimpsing but not really noticing the surroundings, as he was more in tune with the eager looks of some of the patrons who eyed Lydia with similar naughty thoughts. One elderly gentleman was receiving a slap from his equally elderly wife. Escorted to their seats by the efficient, uniformed waiter, Josh, remembering gentlemanly manners, sat after Lydia in a reserved fashion, for the moment without conversation as if potential lovers on a first date.

The waiter returned and broke the ice for them. Placing the coffee cups on the table, he simply said, "Lunch?"

Josh declined politely and Lydia requested a Greek salad. While sipping his coffee, enjoying its warmth, Lydia provided a rundown of the day's itinerary. It was all very business-like, clearly a professional. A professional what? was the question. After spending ten minutes listening to her, focusing on her lips, he was at least a little clearer of the family business element and functionality. It seemed she was one of the original dancers at the club. Simon, having noticed her intelligent attributes, soon promoted her to meeter-and-greeter and discreet go-between for VIPs members and their guests, only introducing those to the classiest, extensively competent girls, dependent on what was requested. Nowadays the family held her in complete trust and high regard.

"Why were you at the house yesterday? It's a bit beyond your remit," Josh asked, in seemingly pure innocence, his mouthing cracking a slight grin.

Lydia appeared thoughtful before answering. She decided that Josh was playing some sort of game.

"Simon suggested it. He wanted a female perspective other than your wife's."

"What did you conclude?"

"You're a player, who's on the lookout for fair game - like a shark, always on the prowl. I'm not fair game. I take who or what I want, whenever I want." She inferred mischievously.

"No comment," Josh quipped back in quick response.

"Definitely a player then," Lydia retorted, following up with "Am I wrong? Have I misinterpreted you?"

"We shall wait and see, won't we treacle?"

"Hmm, a player. Yes, before you ask, I telephoned Simon on the way here and told him you can be trusted. I did not tell him that around attractive women, you may not be - no point; I think you and he are very alike in that regard."

Lydia's salad arrived with a fresh pot of coffee.

Salad and three coffees later, the pair walked into the hotel car park, situated in front of the hotel building. Lydia led the way to a familiar looking green Mini Cooper, unlocking it with the remote key fob, easing herself into the driver's seat. Josh took the front passenger seat, without waiting to be asked.

"Fancy a ride?" she announced, as the car burst into life with a push of the starter button.

"If you insist. I'm always up for it in a tasty jam jar."

The car park barrier raised itself after Lydia paid using the attached auto-payment facility. Lydia gently drove the car out, bearing north. Josh kept silent and merely stared at her slender legs shifting up and down as she confidently drove the Mini through Manchester City

Centre. Lydia occasionally glanced at him and licked her full lips somewhat suggestively. This was either a habit or a game. Josh reckoned he should play the game, and laid his hand on a sleek, stocking-clad leg. She did not remove it or utter a word. Josh took that as encouragement and stroked, taking care not to enter between her warm and inner thighs. Lydia positioned his hand between, but before he could seek further, the Mini screeched to an abrupt halt. Lydia switched off the engine. Josh knew she was teasing him.

"First stop," she said.

A double meaning, decided Josh. He clocked the street name - Coombe Lane -or so he thought as the sign was somewhat vandalised. He also noticed the large group of Cossack-hat-wearing men milling around.

Lydia recommended that he should go in alone, explaining why, and ask for Abe. Abe was a family associate, and his business was a Jewish food supermarket. As Josh opened the car door, she settled a hand firmly between slightly opened legs, smiled seductively, moistening her lips with her tongue, providing extensive sexual eye-contact. Lydia clearly loved to play games.

What a tease, reflected Josh, as he walked through the open shop door.

The store surroundings were not salubrious, in fact they were somewhat scruffy, some would say dirty. How it passed health and safety was another question (Josh concluded that as rodents were not kosher, they would not dare enter). He strolled to the till, stopping to inspect a bottle of olives stacked with various brands on a dusty shelf before spotting a young Jewish man and inquiring as to whereabouts of Abe. The young man was a little hesitant until Josh offered his name. Nervously, he pointed to the back, announcing he could not leave the till unmanned. Josh followed the finger.

The man was slightly older than he, but the lines on Abe's face and receding grey hairline plainly invoked a life of hardship. Josh offered his hand; Abe took it. The handshake was firm and friendly.

"Welcome. Mark telephoned me and said I should expect you."

The ensuing conversation was brief and held in the crowded stockroom. Abe seated himself behind a small tatty untidy desk, littered with small boxes, invoices, and a full ashtray. Josh sat on an uncomfortable-looking chair, finding it was unstable due to one of its legs being substituted with a snooker cue, forcing the occupant to sit and balance.

Josh soon realised the importance of visiting the shop and meeting Abe. After a brief discussion, hands were shaken and Josh walked back outside after purchasing a pack of cigarettes from the young man minding the till. Outside, he lit one, inhaled, looked around and discovered that the Green Mini Cooper was not where he had left it. Using the new iPhone, Josh scrolled down and called Lydia. Her answerphone was the response. He did not bother to leave a voice message. To kill time, he took a closer look at the smart phonebook. It contained all the contact numbers of family members that he met the night before, as well as numbers for what looked like local mini-cab firms and London phone numbers. The phone vibrated in his hand. The screen said Lydia. Josh intentionally pressed the busy key.

Moments later, the car resurfaced and stopped in front of him. Josh jumped into the mini after Lydia opened the passenger door.

"Hey, what took you?" he said. "Where to now?"

Lydia explained that the rest of the drive would primarily be drive-by.

"Give me the 'ed's up on where I should focus me mince pies."

"Yeah. I will do - your eyes appear to be constantly on my thighs."

"That's what 'appens if you pull your skirt up around your waist."

Lydia had adjusted her skirt up, but not to that extent.

"Pervert. Can't a girl get comfortable?" she replied.

"I ain't a perv; you're a flirt - what else am I going to

do with me mince pies?" Lydia and Josh laughed with each other, understanding their mutual tease.

The first "stop and look" was an orthodox synagogue. The building itself had seen better days, but in its prime must have been a handsome addition to the Victorian homes with which it blended. This was where regular family meetings took place each Saturday morning and according to Lydia was a necessity. Luckily for him he would not be expected to attend from London: a Sunday morning call would do. Anything urgent she could handle discretely.

"I bet your good at handling things - the bigger the better."

"No comment," copying what Josh said earlier at breakfast.

Lydia changed tact, asking the blatantly obvious question.

"Are you religious in any way? No disrespect, but you don't strike me that way."

"Err, no. I understand the basics as I was brought up Jewish and snipped at eight days old - and sorry love, you ain't checking."

"I see," she said, concentrating on the road ahead, with a conscious eye on Josh, his hand again resting on her exposed leg.

Josh realised the question was purely to gauge a reaction, and he finished with "I have played with plenty of shiksas."

Lydia pretended not to hear and continued with his extended family history. Josh discovered that only Max was deeply religious, and the others just went along to keep him happy. Apparently the local Jewish community knew this, but as the family supported many charities and kept the right-wingers in check, they were accepted.

Max, out of his own pocket, paid for a new roof after the great storm of '87, and was one of the anti-racist leaders during the heyday of the National Front in the late 1970s. In fact, in those days he often led the demonstrations, and was always the first involved in the violent street battles that often followed when the Front charged. Some of those early battles produced men of character; many long-term family connections were built. Others, straighter, were now in politics, fighting the good fight wherever racist activity raised its ugly head. During tensions, the politicians were contacted, and second-generation soldiers did battle.

Lydia drove skilfully while continuing to feed Josh with history and family dynamics. There were no longer any wise cracks, but the build-up of sexual tension was still clear as Lydia fondled the car switches and occasionally stroked the gear stick suggestively, taking her eyes off the road to watch Josh's reaction. She allowed Josh to keep his hand on her leg, but she would not allow it to stroke, it had to stay still. She pointed out the Thai Massage parlours and guys wearing hoodies and baseball caps on their street corners in the less salubrious areas. The occupants on their corners and inside the parlours did not know their real guvnors. Buffers were always used.

Lydia would not say what had happened to Max's son, except that he had died in Strangeways Prison.

The lessons of history continued, with relevant enterprises pointed out. Josh tried to press for more on Max's sons.

"I know you said Max lost a son, one in prison, but what happened to the other one, David's Father? Rachel won't ever mention his name, except that he's dead to us. It seems odd that neither mother is around, again both never mentioned."

"Look, Josh, I have no idea. It was before my time, and I think perhaps you should not push them. If your wife won't tell you perhaps it's for a good reason. What is it you say? Stay schtum. Perhaps listen to your own advice."

Josh acknowledged Lydia was probably right and turned the subject towards her.

She became coy but gave a not too subtle hint when she simply said, "I like to fuck; you could consider it my hobby."

Josh was not expecting that as an answer as they arrived back at the hotel.

Apartment...

"Josh, it's check out time."

Lydia instructed as they arrived back inside the hotel lobby. Josh looked slightly mystified.

"Err," was Josh's response. He assumed he was here for the duration of the visit.

"Do not worry, we have one extra stop," Lydia said in her sexy, husky voice to a bemused Josh.

Josh said nothing. Lydia took hold of his arm, interlinking with hers, and walked them over to the hotel reception check out.

An elderly lady was at the desk inspecting her bill. Lydia hung onto Josh as they waited, and for no reason began nibbling his neck and moved her arm to his behind, pinching his buttocks hard.

Giggling, she whispered, "That's for last night."

The elderly lady having completed her business strode off muttering something unintelligible under her breath.

"Yes Sir, how can I help?" the camp-sounding receptionist said, raising his dark eyebrows.

"Can I have the bill please? Room 340."

"Of course, Sir. Card or cash?"

"Cash, please," answered Josh.

Lydia, still giggling, leaned on the shiny raised surface, allowing her bosom to rest on the top, giving the receptionist an unwanted eyeful. He again raised his eyebrows at Lydia's attempt at winding him, indicating that single occupancy rooms were for single guests only. Lydia responded by squeezing her breasts together with both hands, staring intently at the receptionist before laughing loudly and turning to Josh, resulting in the receptionist waving his arms around in an actorly kind of way. This was undoubtedly Lydia's intention. Josh was somewhat surprised, as on payment and with a wave of the obviously gay man's hand, his Samsonite suitcase appeared and was placed beside him by an elderly hotel porter. Josh realised this was all pre-planned.

Lydia could not resist a final say after Josh thanked the receptionist.

"Yes, you're right, we fucked all night long and he has a great big cock."

"Lydia come on stop messing about," Josh said, actually slightly embarrassed, especially with a slight hard-on - which he was sure the receptionist had spotted.

Once back in the Mini and after a ten-minute drive they arrived at a smart modern apartment complex. Lydia drove down a clearly signed parking ramp and parked in a bay marked 231. Lydia opened the car's glove box, intentionally brushing Josh's inner leg as she handed him an apartment front door fob and key, clasping his hand longer than necessary.

"We use this apartment for our guests - it's cheaper

and far more private than a hotel," she explained.

Josh could not agree more. The thought of been holed up in a too-clinical hotel room was not his idea of fun. He did wonder, though, what else was on the day's agenda; after all, it was only 7.30 p.m.

He kept pace with Lydia, who strode purposefully towards the clearly marked car park lift leading to the residential apartment block. Lydia acknowledged a middle-aged man already waiting for the arrival of the lift.

The lift doors opened, and both allowed the first patron in. Josh, always a gentleman, gestured for Lydia to enter next. She did so with a polite business type nod. The lift doors closed. They both vacated it on the second floor, leaving the middle-aged man to continue his journey. Josh followed Lydia to door number 231 and unlocked it with the key from the Mini glovebox, allowing Lydia in first.

Behind the apartment door was as you would expect in a modern apartment: an open-plan living space with glass from floor to ceiling, generating sun rays that shot across the apartment, settling on the black marble kitchen work surface.

Josh surveyed the living space which housed a modern beige sofa, matching beige leather armchair surrounding a glass lounge table, assorted magazines stacked neatly in one corner and a black glass ashtray embellished with the Pepper Wilder emblem. He glanced at the forty-four-inch widescreen TV on the only non-glass wall. Other than that, the room was sparsely furnished. There were seven or eight steps beside the small kitchenette to the mezzanine floor. He presumed that was the bedroom. Lydia was busy in the kitchen, preparing drinks after collecting tumblers from a cupboard.

"Single Malt?" she enquired, already knowing the answer.

"Yeah, make mine a double - no ice," Josh responded.

"Who do you think I am, your wife?"

"Nah, me trouble and strife wouldn't ask - she knows the answer."

"Cheeky fucker," she said, handing Josh his malt.

He tried again pressing her for more information on Max's sons. Lydia, still not forthcoming, suggested he "Ask Max."

For the moment they both stood sipping, enjoying the alcohol. Lydia picked up a small remote-control device which was hiding beneath the magazines, pressed a button which produced a slight whirring sound, as previously hidden white blinds emerged, stopping once covering the entire window space. She continually avoided the question of Max's son and talked through their later evening plans: a visit to Pepper Wilder, the main legit part of the business. For the first time today, the conversation was without sexual banter. It appeared they had both turned into shy virgins the instant they entered the lift.

Lydia's mobile rang. It had the old-fashioned ringtone of a 1930s house telephone.

"Yeah OK, laters." She hung up.

Lydia did not divulge who called but said simply, "We have an extra couple of hours to kill. Do you want a bite?" she said, biting her top lip hard.

"Only if you're me dessert. I fancy some Jack and Danny," he responded, lighting a Marlborough.

"You ain't getting mine, you couldn't afford my pussy," she said walking towards the bathroom glass in hand, shooting Josh a provocative backwards glance. She deliberately left the sliding door ajar enough for Josh to see that the bathroom was a wet room with marble decor. She unzipped her tight business skirt and let it fall to the marble floor, revealing a pink thong, and began slowly unbuttoning her beige shirt. Lydia instinctively knew that he was watching and fondled her breasts, pinching a nipple hard, the other hand slipping inside her thong, before closing the bathroom door.

Josh heard her turn the shower on, taking a seat on the beige leather sofa, lighting a second cigarette whilst enjoying his whisky. An image of Lydia formed in his mind: her soaping herself down, utilising the shower head as a toy. After ten minutes, whisky glass now drained and hard with that thought, Josh decided to gate-crash the bathroom as Lydia he assumed, like him, had relinquished the virginal pangs of earlier.

The steam from the rainfall shower formed a silhouette on Lydia's perfectly curved body. Josh removed his clobber as Lydia watched with wide, inviting, take-me-now eyes.

"Make yourself useful. Grab the coconut shower bottle and wash me down. I'm a very dirty girl."

Josh did as requested, stepping in behind her, admiring her perfect form as he massaged the perfumed gel slowly into her back, gradually moving to her behind and upper legs, deliberately brushing her mound with his fingers, avoiding her opening.

"Tease. I'm dirty everywhere, especially here."

"Where's 'ere?"

Lydia took his hands in hers and positioned them over her wet-gel slippery breasts.

"My nipples. Feel them, nip them."

Josh fleetingly did as asked, but only for an instant.

"Foreplay can wait. You're filthy, you told me, you need washing all over."

Josh laughed; Lydia moaned.

He let her stew and worked his way around to her firm gym-worked stomach, his hands and body wet with the hot flowing shower water. Lydia, gasping and begging, guided his hands between her legs. First, her mound, taunting her Brazilian. Her legs widened naturally, allowing access to her opening, wet with water and desire. Her gasping increased, pushing him towards her needs and pleasure. Josh finally played with her full, rounded breasts, his other hand meeting hers in sliding towards her slit, turning to meet his mouth. Josh kissed her delicately at first, his tongue hovering over her lips. Lydia's tongue sought more, greedily beckoning his as he nibbled her lower lip. She responded passionately, drawing his tongue in to explore her mouth. Her nipples hardened as he encircled them slowly with hands and fingers. Her moaning insistent with desire. She turned to face him, tongues dancing to each other's tune. Josh lightly pinched her nipples.

"Harder!" she demanded.

His mouth replaced his fingers, biting her nipples hard. Lydia urged his mouth lower, towards her firm midriff. Josh explored her belly button. Lydia, impatient, pushed him further.

"Eat me, my pussy's yours."

Josh did not disappoint, kissing and massaging her inner thighs, paying attention to the small delicate butterfly tattoo on her left, ignoring in-between. Lydia reached down to his stiff, thick cock, caressing expertly, enjoying the throb of its urgency, fighting with her own urgent need.

Lydia's right hand found the need, fingering her eagerness, forcing her body to jerk into eager splaying fingers. Pussy lips parting, directing Josh's mouth, his tongue obeyed fingers, locating her hard clit and exploring deeper into her womanhood.

"Don't stop, suck me. Fucking eat my pussy, I'm coming." Her husky voice urgent in imminent arrival.

Her body flailed against his mouth as his tongue flicked faster, encircling and tasting her sweet bud. Her hands behind supported her thrusting body against the shower wall. Her inner muscles seized his tongue as she quivered in ecstasy, coming hard but demanded more. Josh instinctively knew. He turned her body, his hardness penetrating its target. Vaginal muscles engulfed and manoeuvred his manhood, her moaning and breathing becoming intense, building, ready to explode again. He cupped her breasts with one hand, his fingers inside her mouth. She sucked at them as they moved as one. She moaned in additional exhilaration as they came together. Josh breathed deeply from the hard sex and said nothing as he stepped beyond the shower after pecking her sex flushed cheek, taking a white bathrobe from the tall, heated towel rail, wrapping it around Lydia as she stepped into his open arms. He patted her body dry before taking the second bathrobe for himself. She smiled.

"I did not realise you were such a gentleman in and out the shower," she said, giggling as she dabbed a white face towel on his lower lip which was gently seeping blood. "Josh, I hope it's doesn't hurt. I was horny I got carried away."

"You're not a vampire, are you?" Josh looked at her

in all seriousness, before cracking up in laughter.

“Yeah, a pussy vampire, obviously,” Lydia said, “and I prefer to cum after dark.”

She looked at him like a contented cat having drunk its cream. Before leaving the wet room, she kissed his mouth hard and blew a kiss towards his still slightly hard cock.

“Not this time,” she said, grinning. “More later if you’re a good cockney.” She wiggled her pert bathrobe-covered arse as she walked out the wet room. With some, but not all, of her sexual energy spent, Lydia sedately sat her firm arse on the sofa, lit, and smoked one of Josh’s cigarettes. Hearing him in the shower, singing was certainly not one of his fortes - however, tongue-use was a different matter. In fact, Lydia decided Josh was first rate in that department. She began to reminisce and relive the shower experience. She certainly was no shy virgin. That was lost whilst still at school with a boy, a sixth former, eighteen months older. It seemed a lifetime ago, even though it often came to mind after intercourse, especially with a new partner. Lydia could not help but play over the image of their shower sex. Hands automatically fondled and teased her breasts, responding rapidly to her touch. Nipples hardening, Lydia's wetness seeped between her legs. Her hand had little choice but to assist, finding her vulva lips unlocking to desire, working her clitoris into a frenzy.

She concentrated on the large cock that fucked her deeply just thirty minutes ago, its girth filling and stretching her mouth. Lydia laid back into the comfortable sofa, her mouth gently sucking at his testicles. Fingers pressed and circled, her love tool widened her legs, clamping on a finger as it found her G-Spot. The organ impaled her eager mouth after she devoured its leaking head. It throbbed as it gushed warm, salty fluid deep into the back of her throat, provoking spasms of lust. Her vision allowing a mix of cum and saliva to seep out. Touching the warm liquid as it trickled down her jaw, erupting twice in quick succession as the cock expended its remaining burden. Finally, she massaged the cum urgently into her breasts, detonating a third, stifling her moans with a hand.

Josh appeared in front of her, bringing Lydia back to reality, wondering if Josh had enjoyed a free private phonographic show: her bathrobe open, exposing her breasts, fingers wet with saliva, legs wide, pussy radiating spent lust.

She had no idea how long Josh had been standing watching, but did she care?

In the past, this was how she earnt a few extra quid, and besides, she was always an extrovert.

"Fancy a nibble?" she offered.

"Sure, why not. I ain't had a bite for ages."

"Josh, Josh, wake up. Hope you like Chinese. It's in

front of you."

Lydia's voice startled him. The meal stirred his senses, Josh realised he had

been napping. There also was only one serving and Lydia was fully clothed.

"Where's your nosh? Ain't you hungry after your - I mean our - workout?"

Lydia was not but needed to leave for a fresh change of clothing available in her own apartment.

Josh let her leave, without further conversation, he also discovered the Mini keys on the glass table.

"Weird," he muttered out loud.

His thoughts drifted towards the day's events. It had certainly been a long day, and he smiled to himself at the thought of earning proper regular money and having a satisfactory purpose.

Young Lydia

He was still not 100% sure of what his role would actually be. Whilst munching on his meal, his mind went through various theories as to what it meant. The Marks and Sparks £15 Meal Deal was actually tastier than expected. Josh had not heard the kitchen microwave - good sex can induce heavy sleep in a man. For some reason the last bite compelled Josh to think of his wife Rachel. He picked up the iPhone and scrolled through the address book. His London number and Rachel's mobile were under "Granddaughter". It was likewise listed on the speed-dial. He changed "Granddaughter" to "Trouble and strife", adding a siren ringtone under edit before attempting to phone her, but the number was busy. This surprised him, as he remembered it was book club night and half expected Rachel to still be there. He hit the number 3 button again. This time the phone connected. Rachel answered on the third ring and replied in her usual loud but slightly sleepy voice, in a tone that she usually reserved for her slightly angrier moments. On hearing her husband's voice her response became affectionate. Josh was (even though slightly annoyed that she was on the telephone when he first dialled), deep down, pleased to hear her voice. He did love her, even though he did not always show it. He also suspected she was aware of his various indiscretions but, providing he did not take it home with him metaphorically, she never questioned him.

"Hi," she said, "how are things at home? How's the family?"

"They all send their love."

Josh hated these little exchanges, as they sounded so Jewish, and unlike his own dysfunctional family. He was probably just jealous. Rachel's family were close-knit, unlike his own. They continued with their small talk until Rachel spoke of the family's offer. This surprised him; it meant she was aware. Their exchange also offered the impression that she had somewhat instigated the meeting - well, at least suggested it. Rachel, an only granddaughter, knew how to manipulate in order to get her own way. Josh's position within the family assisted her and more importantly, the occasional begging phone call for monetary help would become a thing of the past. Josh was sure she did that when things got tight. He was also convinced that Rachel would soon return to her habit of peeking into estate agent windows and perhaps even sign up. Jewish wives preferred to show off at least two bathrooms and a double garage. Their home only had the one bathroom and no garage.

Meanwhile, unknown to Josh, Lydia arrived at her own apartment two minutes after they parted. Hers was in the next building in the same smart development. Lydia did think about mentioning it, but for the moment decided against it. Her employers instructed her to look after Josh.

Simon had specified "if you want to fuck him, fuck him, but Max must never know". It was not a secret that she suffered nymphomaniacal tendencies. Josh certainly knew what he was doing and clearly was adept at pressing her excessive buttons. Lydia hoped this would be allowed to continue.

This was not always the case. Her emotions drifted to her past, hurt memories flooded back. The feelings dwelled in her mind on entering her plush, but perhaps too sparse, bedroom. She opened the walk-in wardrobe and started looking through her evening wear. Flicking through the dresses, she came across her first teenage ballet outfit. Tears followed.

Life had started well for her. She was from a good, stable family living on the outskirts of Manchester in a semi-, her father working his way up from factory assembly worker to floor manager and, eventually, shop steward, looking after eight hundred men. Keeping workers and management happy through the recession of the early '90s was no mean feat. Happiness continued until the eve of her twelfth birthday, when her doting father died in a head-on collision with youths from Moss Side driving a stolen BMW. Lydia's mother had tried and succeeded for a time, until the help from the union dried up, her father's pension only barely covering the ever-increasing mortgage payments. Her mother eventually gave up and handed the house back to the bank, ending up in a high-rise on the wrong side of Manchester, rubbing further salt into family wounds. Her elder brother managed to get out and gained a promotion in the British Army, based in Germany. Lydia was not so lucky: with little money available, the dancing lessons her father paid for in advance did not last beyond a year. In fact, the very outfit she was now holding was a birthday present from that fateful day. She sobbed profusely as she continued thinking about that dark period.

On leaving school without a qualification to her name, she drifted from dead-end job to dead-end job. Dancing saved her. She always took care of herself and her looks, eating sensibly and keeping fit, even if it meant just running up and down the stairwells on the estate. This was where her virginity was taken by the sixth former, who finished within a minute of removing her knickers. He had come before removing his own jeans, but she soon got him hard again due to her natural ability. She spat his cum out, initially in fright, but moments later gained confidence in her ability to please and relished the throbbing cock probing her mouth.

She had first begun dancing for wages in a nightclub, dressed in skimpy tight latex, doing her thing in a black cage hanging from the dark recess of the venue with spotlights following her every move. The idea was to animate the clubbers to dance below. Naturally, all below gazed up in awe, the lights creating a silhouette, conveying the impression of almost nude dancing. The eagle-eyed noticing her lack of knickers. Only a few months into the job, Lydia suggested to management that she share the cage with another woman, creating further interest. This provoked her own same-sex interest in such a confined tight space when her first dance partner became very hands-on, discovering her lack of knickers, leading to her first orgasm from another woman, up there in the relative darkness. Not like her first threesome, with a VIP male patron who later joined them at the bar, interrupting their alcohol-induced snog and inviting them "back to his place" for privacy.

Lydia could pinpoint that precise moment to the onset of her nymphomania.

The double-dancing also provided an acceptable pay increase.

Lydia's eyes dried and her mouth cracked into a smile as her reflections continued. For it was on the dancing podium that night, and the early-hours threesome that she realised her liberal sexuality could be used to control if she wanted or required it.

Her dancing prowess led to bottom-end pole dancing clubs and all the extras an entrepreneurial woman could make on the side, where the real money could be made. It was here where she continued to enjoy sex with both sexes, becoming more experimental, daring and extrovert, leading to wild sex parties and orgies often held in the wealthiest large private homes. The money sometimes became secondary; some would say she had developed a problem. One friend even suggested she was a sex addict, handing her a shrink's business card after one such event led to Lydia having all the house revellers by dawn. Lydia, at a previous engagement, was recommending numbers on a card handed to each individual. All who held an even number card could do as desired to her. Lydia made the game more interesting by wearing a blindfold. Perhaps she was a sex addict. Once or one was never enough. The sexual thoughts began to make her horny again. It was at one of those discreet parties that she first met Gary, who later organised a birthday bash at the family club. Everyone wanted, at the very least, to talk to her - many had her. She was the honey to the bees that night. Gary quickly realised her potential, as she was perfectly capable of holding a conversation, be it political, business or a TV Soap. Within eight months of joining Pepper-Wilder, she retired from draping herself around poles and was promoted to management of the dancers.

Her reminiscing stopped when she found the perfect red mini dress for the evening. Lydia, as usual, spent time choosing underwear. It was all top end, Agent Provocateur. She felt good slipping the dress over her head, after checking her appearance underneath: revealing white strapless bra, stockings, suspender belt, and open-crotch knickers. Lydia was fully aware that with the right light her undergarments would be seen. Dabbing her usual Chanel No. 5 on her neck, wrists, and between her thighs, enjoying the slight sharpness perfume offered in private areas, she shuddered slightly. Her ritual complete, she headed for the front door.

Whilst Lydia was having her horny moment, Josh was continuing his conversation with his wife.

He was slightly coy with his next question.

"What do you mean?" he said, trying to hide his surprise that she knew something, at the very least.

"Zayde tells me everything."

Josh thought she sounded even more like a Jewish Princess. She was beginning to piss him off, as he hated it when she played the favourite Granddaughter, especially when she used Yiddish terms. Because of his silence, she spoke again before he had answered.

"How's Lydia, the attractive black girl?" Josh almost choked on his scotch.

"Sorry, love," regaining his composure. "I met her at the family dinner - she was one of the waitresses. I saw her name tag. She seems to know her place. I think she works at the club; Simon sort of suggested that was the case."

This pacified Rachel and she changed the subject.

"Zayde said something to me a couple of months ago; he told me there might be an opening for you."

Josh, assuming she must know something, tried

one more question, whilst lighting a Marlborough.

She again played the Jewish Princess and became equally coy.

"I gather your running the family business interests down here and traveling regularly to Manchester. Are you in the apartment yet?"

Josh decided she knew very little and was now playing the gangster moll, using lines from her favourite old movie.

"Yeah, it's blinding, ace view. Have to go love, you know what Max – sorry, I mean your grandfather's like. See you soon, miss you."

He hung up, but not before hearing her blow her usual kisses down the phone.

He tugged on the remainder of his cigarette and briefly thought of their last outing. It was a "Gangster and Moll" evening held at one of his hangouts. All the guests were dressed as roaring '20s gangsters, with the men in checked three-piece suits, set off with pocket watches or Tommy guns and women wearing flapper dresses. Rachel was certainly no Jewish Princess that night.

He stubbed his smoke out in the Pepper Wilder ashtray.

Introducing Pepper Wilder...

The intercom buzzed. Josh checked his appearance in the bathroom mirror, expecting Lydia. He answered on the second buzz and viewed the small video screen. He recognised the grainy image as Stumpy grinning up at him.

"Do you wanna come up?"

Josh checked his new Rolex while waiting for Stumpy's answer. The watch face said 10:45.

"I'll see you outside. I'm in the black S-Class," Stumpy replied, curtly.

Josh swiftly emptied his glass and placed it in the sink of the galleried kitchen. He picked up the front door keys that were by the ashtray and left through the apartment's front door.

Josh strolled out the lift on the ground floor, acknowledging the concierge with a nod of his head, as he left via the main door that was directly in front of the concierge desk. Once out of the building he spotted the S-Class Mercedes parked up on his left, the engine purring in anticipation of its journey. Josh was somewhat surprised, as Stumpy occupied the rear of the vehicle and a youngish man in a black suit was sitting behind the wheel. On seeing Josh, the driver jumped out and like a flash of lighting, opened the passenger door. Josh got in and sank down into the sumptuous leather upholstery.

"'Ello mate," Josh said, clicking the seatbelt into place.

Stumpy's response was warm and had none of the animosity he had showed during their first encounter. He explained to Josh that the journey was only a ten-minute ride, and that the S-Class was usually reserved for VIPs visiting Pepper Wilder.

"Where's the Yiddo clobber?" Josh jokingly enquired, as Stumpy was dressed immaculately in what looked like a made-to-measure, dark blue three-piece suit. He was also sporting a trimmed beard, darker than before.

Josh himself was smart, but more casual in appearance, wearing a good fitting Ben Sherman 'Slim-fit'.

"That clobber, as you say, is for grafting and keeping the old man happy. Religious nuts can get away with murder. It was originally Joseph's idea."

"Joseph?" Josh asked.

"Yeah," Stumpy had let something slip and was slightly lost for words.

Josh, sensing his opportunity, pushed further and took an educated guess.

"His son and heir?"

"Yeah, yeah, but it didn't come from me."

Josh decided that Stumpy was not a true Mancunian, as his accent definitely changed whilst under pressure.

"A 'saaf' London boy, are you? Tell me more. Us

Londoners should stick together, even if you are from the wrong side of the river!"

Stumpy grimaced as they were interrupted (and in Stumpy's case rescued) by a large, suited black man who opened the car passenger door.

Neither occupant of the Mercedes had seen they had arrived at the club. Josh stepped out the Mercedes, thanked the man who was clearly a doorman-cum-bouncer, lit a cigarette, and took in his new surroundings whilst pondering on his recent conversation.

Pepper Wilder was displayed in similar fashion to the ashtray in the apartment, just larger and lit up, looking garish, above the main double doors which were attached to what looked like railway arches. The arches took up most of the badly lit street; but adorned with a design of a pepper pot and a wildebeest with a naked lady astride it in blue, just as his Zippo lighter was. Josh also noted the well-dressed girls almost huddled together at the other end of the premises above a neon sign that said "Exit". Clearly club working girls, enjoying a smoke before work.

"Evening Josh," said Gary, as Josh ground his cigarette into the uneven, old-fashioned cobbled pavement.

Josh extended a hand, which was shaken in a firm, but friendly, way.

Gary led his brother-in-law into the venue. Josh was slightly surprised by his surroundings, as the club was a lot classier than he had anticipated. The bar area was a semi-circle, with staff behind and around it dressed in a sophisticated but erotic way. Leather topped stools with chrome legs were situated around the bar, with a few suited gentlemen seated on them, facing away from the bar, watching dancers gyrate to the house tunes. They danced, doing their own thing, with a hand between legs, or caressing ample cleavage to the beat. The dancers were all in a state of undress except for thongs leaving little to the imagination. Some at the bar focussed on the dancer appearing to masturbate her chrome pole. Poles were placed at various points around the club all allowing a 360-degree view. Black leather sofas were dotted around with tables between them for drinks, topped with blue menus standing up complete with the now-familiar Pepper Wilder emblem. Cocktail waitresses mingled around looking sensuous (some clearly bored) in matching leather miniskirts with cropped silky tops, accentuating their sexuality, attending to punters when required. Josh also saw that not all the punters were men; some were of the fairer sex who were also plainly enjoying themselves. One nicely dressed female patron in a tight blue pencil skirt appeared to be slyly touching herself whilst gyrating to the movements of the masturbating pole dancer, her hand inside her skirt as she focused on the extremely erotic dancer.

Josh watched Simon at the other end of the bar,

attending to a distinguished-looking elderly man who was gesticulating wildly with both arms outstretched, clearly finding it difficult to make himself understood – or perhaps simply heard above the modern sound system. Simon, dressed in a purple suit with a matching shirt open at the collar, with a large gold Star of David hanging from an equally thick gold chain. He beckoned over a twenty-something brunette who was busy on her pole and whispered in her ear. She pulled a slightly unimpressed face, leaning back and giving rise to her already large chest appearing, but agreed to his request. The brunette yanked the man's outstretched hand, almost in resentment, and led him towards an ornate stairway resembling the stairwell of the Queen Mary's First Class entertaining lounge. Gary explained to Josh that "upstairs is for VIP guests only." Josh's eyes followed the brunette and the distinguished gent as they climbed the curved carpeted stairs, passing the silver framed photos of scantily clad dancers - some with well-known A-listers.

Josh was distracted by Lydia, who appeared to be floating towards him with a look of anger on her pretty face. She had watched the kerfuffle unfold from her office, situated discretely away from the small private curtained booths, for it held screens of the club's expensive CCTV, including coverage of the extra private booths. Lydia's office was the only place to access coverage of the booths, differing slightly from the security room, which held only the standard coverage. A useful tool in keeping order and providing extra fun for her when time allowed.

Lydia ignored Josh as she climbed down the remaining steps, not even looking in his direction, but moulding a purposeful expression on her face with body language to match, giving the impression of a scolded cat. She marched straight up to Simon.

"Why are you giving another freebee to that old Rabbi?"

Simon grimaced, as he remembered his last heated discussion with Lydia about this particular client. Without religious attire, the distinguished man fitted in as a usual punter. In fact, he did not even look Jewish, but he did have a reputation amongst the club's dancers and the lower-end streetwalker market. He rarely paid the full agreed price but also had an added reputation for having "octopus's hands," which would be less problematic if he paid the required price first.

Lydia again asked the same question, but now more forcefully. Josh was sure he saw a faint teasing smile on her face, but rightly assumed this was for Simon's benefit.

"What do you expect me to do? At this moment I have no choice: I have to keep the old man sweet; you know why, Lydia."

"Simon, this has to be the last time he gets a freebie. He grumbles, and you always give in to him. Is he really that important? Perhaps it's time we just used his son."

"Okay, Lydia, you are probably right. I will bring it up at our next board meeting."

Always with the last word when it came to protecting her girls, Lydia retorted, "You'd better." She was only looking after her stable, who were constantly complaining about this punter.

"I'll pay the girls fully myself, out of my own pocket. Will that keep them happy? As you know, he's important to us."

Lydia smiled and accepted the gesture, knowing exactly who this punter was and his usefulness to the family. Lydia, though finished for now, intended to bring the subject up at the next board meeting, after being voted on unanimously at the last quarterly "sit-down".

Simon gave her a subtle peck on the cheek and turned to Josh and said, "Do you remember Lydia? She served us dinner the other day."

Before he had time to answer, Lydia responded with one of her usual wisecracks.

"Yeah, sweetie, I was the only black girl serving and for some reason, you could not keep your eyes off my butt or my tits."

Josh responded and said, "That's what me mince pies are for. What else would you suggest? And in that little red mini-dress I can see even more, including the white kit underneath."

"It's not for you sweetie - you couldn't afford me. I

dress this way for myself."

"But it looks like your nipples are pleased to see me," Josh fired back. "If I get any closer, they'll blind me."

Simon, bored with the banter, did not see or hear them teasing one another with mutual suggestive looks as they conversed. He was also in total ignorance that a couple of hours earlier they were both happily fucking, as he was occupied with issuing orders to Stumpy through a discreet lapel microphone which Josh had not seen earlier. With the issue temporarily resolved with the Rabbi and Lydia, Simon suggested to Josh that perhaps a chat upstairs in the VIP area was sensible - after all, there was more to discuss, and it was likely that the other in-laws may join them later. Simon made eye contact with the brunette pole dancer who was still with the rabbi, both enjoying a drink at the bar. The brunette understood Simon's eye contact, the signal allowing the Rabbi to put his octopus hands around her slender waist and wherever else they explored, but discretely, within the semi-circle bar. She cleverly ordered another round for both, as she had experienced the gent before and knew a few more drinks would quell his sexual thirst.

Josh followed Simon's lead up the stairwell.

Up Top...

On reaching the top Josh was once again surprised and further impressed by the quality and ambience of the VIP area. He continued to follow Simon, passing a door that said "PRIVATE OFFICE" in large capital letters, noticing an array of private booths: some expansive marked by drawn, dark drapes, undoubtedly occupied with randy punters and dancers offering blowjobs at £150 a go. The unoccupied booths were open to view, in contrast with their neighbours, and had different themed furnishings. Simon took the open booth, seemingly the largest and the furthest away from the private office. The booth was Parisian in its furnishings with four solid wood framed chairs in jute fabric upholstery. At the centre, a table, homogeneous in design; bare, with the exception of a menu detailing drinks and various services on offer standing beside a Pepper Wilder ashtray.

An Art Deco floor lamp stood close by, with just enough space for a dancer to tease a client into submission in parting with cash for their erotic adventure.

"Take a seat Josh, the others will be up soon," Simon proffered.

He sat down and picked up the menu, more for show rather than anything else, and began to read its contents: "Drinks: Whisky, Irish, American; 10 year, or 15 Year Malt."

Simon placed the menu face down on the table dismissively and said the others will be here momentarily. A cocktail waitress, average-height, who had watched them entering the booth ventured in, knowing Simon was one of her bosses, and said, "Can I help you, gents, what's your poison?" Her accent was heavy Mancunian, but with enough Pakistani to give her heritage away, as did her piercing dark eyes, accentuated by her matching makeup. Simon recognised her and responded.

"A bottle of 25 years Glenfiddich, please Aisha - and you're looking well." Josh nodded at Simon's choice. Aisha bent down slightly and stood the menu back up on the table, enabling Josh a view of her muscled upper thighs and a flash of her behind covered in blue knickers.

Aisha, straightening herself up, replied, "Of course, Sir. How many glasses?"

"Four, please."

Aisha nodded an acknowledgment and pulled the drapes shut as she left the booth.

David emerged before Aisha had reached the bar with their order, feeling fresh in his crisp sharp suit. Regrettably for him it was similar to Stumpy's finery. The penguin wobbled in, close behind, drawing the curtain back wider than David as if to make an entrance. Unlike the other three, he was shabbily dressed in an ill-fitting suit. Josh rightly perceived tonight would be a business meeting, not a "lads' night out," mixing with party girls.

David expressed his regret, directing his apology towards Josh for not welcoming him earlier, but explained business had taken him away and Stumpy needed guidance on an urgent matter. He assured Josh that all was well. The penguin just kept quiet, apart from his heavy breathing.

Aisha returned with the 25-year-old Glenfiddich before any real conversation had commenced, with crystal cut tumblers, a Pepper Wilder ice bucket, and water for flavouring purposes only - all to be dispensed from a silver tray. She proceeded to fill the four glasses with the golden-brown liquid, moving around each of them as a good waitress should, filling Simon's glass last. Josh glimpsed that she leaned into Simon slightly too closely for her job description and assumed he was giving her one, especially as Simon's hand disappeared inside her short cocktail skirt for a short moment, seemingly oblivious to the other two. He retrieved a £50 note from a large bundle in his inside jacket pocket and playfully placed it inside her tight top, brushing a clearly erect nipple in the process. The waitress left with a happy smile on her face. Bosses did not pay for their own booze and she knew Simon would be visiting her later with more than just a tip. In fact, she looked forward to playing with his other tip later in the discreet apartment he had set her up in six months ago.

Stumpy...

Stumpy pulled out of a supermarket car park a mile from home after receiving orders from Simon an hour earlier. He was in an elderly Ford Focus that had been supplied by a family acquaintance for the purpose of his current task. The Ford was wearing a set of cloned registration plates lifted from a similar model. He was on an important mission: his twelfth with the family that had taken pity on him and seen his worth whilst at his lowest ebb. His life, up until that point, had been straightforward, that is to say until his last fight. Stumpy had been a reasonably successful prize-fighter with an edge. This edge was actually his old, deceased manager, who had an uncanny ability to bet right, helped by Stumpy's preference for throwing a fight when required. A larger purse always did the trick. His last fight had gone the usual way with Stumpy appearing to struggle to stay on his feet, then, at the right moment, delivering a swift left and right hook, finishing with an uppercut. He laid his opponent out for the count and beyond, resulting in a visit to the local hospital. Unfortunately, this somewhat upset the opposition's corner, who let loose with weapons, some concealed, others making use of whatever came to hand. The old dockside warehouse turned into a bloodbath as the majority of attendees got busy. By the time the local boys in blue arrived, his long-term manager and friend was deceased, his head adequately caved in, the serious damage inflicted by a large baseball bat known as "Billy Nails," named by its owner, a member of the long-established Romany Boxing family who had inflicted the final, fatal blow. Naturally, under the circumstances the family felt aggrieved by their shafting.

Stumpy was given five years, with the owner of "Billy Nails" receiving a term of no less than fifteen years. Stumpy served his term in Strangeways Prison in an open wing, due firstly to the skills of his Queen's barrister, luckily provided and partly contributed by the high-class prostitute who he drove for and fucked occasionally, generally looking after her every need while she worked: be it full-on girlfriend experience or parties with businessmen close to closing major financial deals. Erotic ladies were an aphrodisiac to some, especially the more lascivious, who nine times out of ten held the pen on signing major contracts, especially if further fun was merely hinted at upon signing.

It was during one of these events that the introductions to Lydia were made, both not knowing that eventually, they would share the same boss. His mother, alive at the time and his only living relative, happened to be severely disabled, living in a Jewish home close to the prison. It was argued successfully by his extremely competent barrister that it was a necessity that he served at Her Majesty's Pleasure, close by. The gullible judge approved it, to the surprise of the crown court gallery. It was here that he first met Joseph. He and Joseph were on the same wing and cell neighbours. Stumpy was engaged quietly by the family, as his activities had not gone unnoticed, becoming Joseph's bodyguard, prison confidant, and eventual friend.

Hot Dogging & Fire...

The drive through Manchester was uneventful. He drove carefully and stuck to the speed limit, observing all traffic lights and stop signs, for he knew a handgun (a Walther PPK, nice and lightweight) was sitting snuggly in the glovebox, placed there by a trusted family associate. This way he could at least plead ignorance of its existence, for he was, after all, in a stolen Ford. He took the orbital M60 and drove onto the M62 towards Leeds - an hour's journey if driving at a steady speed. Stumpy pulled off the Leeds Junction and drove towards the sign that said "Leeds West". Stumpy felt the sweat as it spread down his neck as the destination got closer. He passed Leeds Football club, observing the street girls plying their trade, many wearing what he called cheap whore skirts and tops. The instant thought of quick gratification produced a hard-on, especially a blowjob followed by a whore sitting astride him on the passenger seat with hands greedily kneading tits as she rode his manhood. For a split second, he thought about stopping to service his need - fortunately, his head took over, knowing he was in a stolen vehicle and his already in place alibi could be contested later. Stumpy culled the car's engine a stone's throw from the Elland Road Industrial Estate, stepped out of the vehicle and checked for CCTV and occupants in the cars parked. He saw one that was occupied, due to the steamed-up windows, which did not help his amorous thoughts, returned to the Ford and drove the final 150 yards to the industrial estate's entrance.

He killed the lights on the Ford as it drew to a stop close to the entrance of the Estate and the saloon door of a grotty public house. Retrieving the black handgun from the glove box and checking it was loaded, he slid the safety release to “off”. Stumpy was slightly irritated as the weapon’s silencer was not supplied as promised. He made a mental note to report back to the family. Nonetheless, he placed the weapon on the passenger seat and covered it with a current edition of the Manchester Echo. He sat back and relaxed, having tuned the car radio into Manchester FM. It was playing his favourite track, “Wild Horses” by the Rolling Stones. The track was on its final chorus when the target appeared from the saloon door of the pub. He confirmed the man’s identity by checking the image on his iPhone. Pleased the image matched, he pressed the delete button. The man was short and slim, and besides his inebriated state carried an air of arrogance. Stumpy checked his rear-view mirror for civilians and any CCTV he may have missed earlier, hand in readiness to grab the Walther sitting snugly under the newspaper. The man the family knew as the Turk, but unknown to Stumpy, walked drunkenly towards the driver’s door of the Ford. At the right moment Stumpy slung open his door and caught his target just right. Without a murmur but with a look of both pain and surprise etched on his face, the man fell into a heap unconscious on to the tarmac. Stumpy eased himself out of the car, bent over and checked the unconscious man. He was out cold. Once satisfied the gun was not required (which was a bit of luck due to the lack of silencer) he moved to the rear of the Ford and opened the boot. It was empty except for the red petrol can, Stumpy shook it as he expected it to be full. He lifted the Turk easily and placed him next to the red petrol can. Stumpy, after closing the boot, returned to the car driver's seat. Turning the ignition key, the engine kicked into life and he drove through the industrial estate's exit as he did not want to risk reversing down a one-way street. The gun, unused, was returned to the glovebox as weapons were expensive and could be sold at a profit if unfired.

Stumpy was not aware of the man's crime, which was the way he preferred to work when dealing with family business. The Turk's crime was cutting cocaine with too much Paracetamol, which killed three young university students, one boy and two girls, leaving another on life support. The girls' angelic faces were plastered onto the front page of the Manchester Echo, which had naturally upset the Manchester club scene, the University campus, and, of course, the local old bill. The Turk was offered a chance; he was asked politely, but firmly, to reimburse all involved for loss of earnings and get the contaminated drugs off the street. The deadline had passed, with him not only ignoring the gentle reminder, but continuing to peddle the same batch to lesser clientele. The Turk made the call himself that whores were of less value and sold his product to the streetwalkers by Leeds Football Club. He had evidently been supplying the girls who plied their trade here. A local madam, somewhat peeved at the loss of several of her girls, informed Lydia of the goings on after Lydia complained about the lightness of the brown envelopes collected weekly on the family's behalf. The family were equally peeved that the Turk took their earners lives too lightly. Pussy was pussy, whatever end of the market it traded. The madam was on the family payroll, her usual duties were to look out for gentlemen who liked a bit more than the usual handjob: a fuck, or unprotected oral sex, or perhaps sometimes boys. Some of the gents could have opened themselves up for blackmail, especially married men who enjoyed same-sex fun once in a while. The family, once informed, persuaded those considered at risk to enjoy themselves in safer surroundings i.e., the club. None were disappointed.

Stumpy continued his journey until reaching a known dogging and prostitution site by a small pond flanked with trees and a loose gravel car park. He parked away from a parked estate car between trees, which afforded him a view and privacy, having already turned his engine and headlights off. Stumpy left his car to gain a front seat view and intently watched the scene by the estate car unfold. Several men were clearly pleasuring themselves as another dogger was pumping a woman ferociously, her backside protruding out of her passenger door window. She was groaning and screaming in pleasure, which intensified the surrounding wanking. The man pleasuring her withdrew and another took over. After each man had his turn, she opened her car door and spread her legs, her body dressed in only a microskirt. Stumpy, with his own hard-on, continued to watch as she turned to face her audience. She proceeded to touch herself. One man offered to help her out with his own fingers inside her, another fondled her breasts. Two others continued to wank. The dogging woman shooed the two away and gestured to the other two. They obliged as she went down on one, while stroking the other's cock. The cock's owner was allowed the first prize of eating her pussy out as she continued to suck the other. Roles changed at her leisure. This continued until all were spent. The men wandered off. The female driver dressed outside her car, got in and drove off.

Stumpy waited approximately ten minutes before he continued with his own business. He opened his car door and stepped out of the Ford, walked to the back of it, and lifted the boot open. The Turk was still out cold. He felt for a pulse; there wasn't one, but he did note the blood seeping from the now deceased Turk's mouth and left ear. Stumpy chuckled to himself, as he realised the tarmac was harder than it looked. He removed the red petrol can from the car boot, and after seating his dead victim in the rear seat, unscrewed the cap and poured petrol over the corpse. Stumpy removed the car's fuel cap, and after opening the right rear door, poured petrol over the rear seat. He retrieved the handgun from the glovebox and the newspaper from the passenger seat, and with his gold zippo lit the newspaper. Once the flame took hold, he threw it onto the rear seat after opening the rear window. Shutting the door, Stumpy watched as the fire grew, taking him slightly by surprise by its intensity.

Fall Girl...

Removing his mobile phone from his jacket, he dialled a number from memory. The call connected to the helpful madam, who to Stumpy was just a voice. She in turn phoned her contact at the local police station and explained that one of her girls was arguing with a punter and that it was going a bit too far. This poor girl was the fool girl. Her over-use of drugs and drink had destroyed her and made her usefulness as even a "brass" unattainable. The police soon picked her up and charged her, at the scene. A few hours deprived of drugs at the police station resulted in an easy confession when offered a hit.

Case closed.

The police, happy with the quick result and the death of the Turk, especially given his links to the dead students, considered it an all-round result.

Escape? Not Me, Gov....

Stumpy walked slowly away from the scene, finishing his call, feeling the heat of the fire on his back. He stuck to the shadows, avoiding the whores who appeared drawn to the fire like flies around shit. Again, he did not know it, but this included the fall girl. He walked back the way he had driven in, relaxing as he moved further from the scene. He heard the distinct sound of a fire engine and police vehicles as he neared the main road at this point and he booked an Uber, tapping in his destination, Ascot Grange, a business hotel on the Otley Road.

The Uber arrived in three minutes. The journey, about a mile, took eight minutes and was completed in silence. Stumpy ignored the driver's small talk. This was to help ensure the driver would not remember him, should an unlikely problem arise. Stumpy entered the four-star hotel lobby - making sure he was seen on arrival - and soon found the bar. Ordering a light beer and chatting to the friendly barman, he began drinking at a steady pace. On ordering a second beer he borrowed the barman's phone after explaining his phone's battery was flat and telephoned a local minicab.

"How much to Manchester Piccadilly?" he asked politely.

The unseen female voice quoted a price. Stumpy

agreed after a little haggling. He did not expect to get a discount, but haggling was a duty. After finishing his second beer and downing a chaser, he bid goodbye to the attentive barman.

Leaving the bar, and waiting in the semi-covered smoking area, he lit a cigarette.

Playtime - or Not...

The night was better fun than Josh had anticipated, the Penguin thankfully only giving a brief summary of his expected duties in London. Josh would sort of be in charge, which as far as he could tell meant keeping a sharp eye on the staff - one in particular, who seemed to be constantly stirring up trouble with the few Muslim staff members directly employed in the London warehouse. It was stressed that these members of staff were bullied; racism was deemed unacceptable by Max. Josh's other and main important role was to keep their elderly London Rabbi sweet. The Rabbi was there solely to check on the kosher wine bottles and other kosher products, basically ensuring packaging was correct and the products were indeed kosher complete, with correct labelling, but abundantly clear tampering had not taken place during the journey from Israel. He was paid well above the going rate for this service, including turning a blind eye to other aspects of the business. The family thought that humorous, as the Rabbi only enjoyed partial sight. The Rabbi, with the family's blessing, employed his oldest son to oversee his work, blessing the odd crate that his father missed due to the old man's reliance on his whisky-filled hip flask, both unaware the goods that came into the warehouse via the Thames already had extra product added. This crucial part of the business was carried out quietly elsewhere by handpicked employees only. Josh was also expected to shadow the delivery vehicles journey to Manchester to the main distribution hub, Abe's premises, on a monthly basis. Simon continued with other business aspects, including London clubs and restaurants. The Penguin, bored of the business chat, wobbled off after a new dancer caught his eye, or was it the chocolate flake she was licking suggestively? David broke the monotonous chat by jokingly asking if the Penguin desired the chocolate or the dancer, as chocolate was a big "no no," especially since his recent diagnosis of diabetes. After much laughter at the Penguin's expense, Simon confirmed the whereabouts of the London premises, in Limehouse, in an old undeveloped area just off the Commercial Road. A printing company, based in South London, close to Millwall Football Club, produced the required labels. Simon also informed Josh that Monday morning he may be travelling down the M1 to London. Josh was instructed to spend a couple of weeks with Rachel on paid leave before officially starting, but that said leave would perhaps involve a quiet site visit during that period. Until Sunday night he could enjoy himself on the club's expense account. David, briefly interrupting, pointed out that he would be expected at Max's Synagogue on Saturday morning, and out of respect was expected to be sober and not smell of pussy. The statement amused Josh as it was abundantly clear the men of the family took pleasure with gentiles, and none of the nice Jewish wives had any idea. Pepper Wilder was also off the menu on Friday night. Nice Jewish boys stayed in for the Sabbath and were not expected to be seen on the street. What they did in the privacy of their own hotel or apartment was another matter. Naturally, Lydia would be available to cater to his every need.

Simon smirked at Josh when he mentioned Lydia and said, "She's told us about your earlier fun and games as you would expect; don't worry, Max does not know, and he never will." He then came out with the typically corny line: "What happens in Pepper Wilder stays in Pepper Wilder."

They all laughed.

Playing with Club Toys...

Stumpy reappeared, grinning from ear to ear. His appearance somewhat dishevelled, Josh put this down to the two scantily clad dancers, one on each arm. One held a small leather whip. Josh assumed that Stumpy had been enjoying himself in one of the other booths.

Mercedes Nelson was the dancer on Stumpy's right arm. She was his favourite and would perform for him on a regular basis, as she had a soft spot for the big man. He always treated her with respect and would often award her with expensive gifts. The soft spot did not stem from his sexual prowess as he was lacking in that department, possessing only a small penis. Some of the girls suggested that this was the real reason for the nickname Stumpy. Usually after Stumpy had completed important business (as he often put it) he required unusual sexual games. Mercedes's sixth sense told her today was such an occasion. Stumpy was not aware that the favours he received were given to him at a price paid for by the family. She felt she was in a "win-win" situation. Mercedes also believed in time that she may be able to turf that bitch Lydia off her perch. In her view, Lydia had passed her sell-by-date.

She felt good, she was dressed in her sexiest evening wear. The blue micro-dress hugged her body tightly, emphasising her rounded bottom and new tits: a gift after

Stumpy's last bit of work. The club, professional, dark and sultry in demeanour, radiated sexuality to the boys in the booth. Attached to Stumpy's left arm was her dancing partner in crime. This lady, Vamp (her club name), was dressed similarly, but her slim body was encased tightly in black latex. Her complexion was pale, even vampire-like in its whiteness. They were exquisite together and the most sought-after act in the club. It helped that they were bisexual lovers, and it would often show through in their performance. The old Rabbi had actually described them as total heathen sluts.

Stumpy acknowledged those seated and took the Penguin's chair and whisky as the two girls positioned themselves behind him.

Lydia, as Simon hoped, appeared as Stumpy replenished only his glass from the table bottle, having adjusted her makeup and added a fresh dab of perfume from a bottle in her office. She was making it clear she was not happy, as all eyes were on Mercedes and her lover who were engrossed in each other's bodies as they worked the booth, enjoying each other's caress, both becoming more intense as eyes concentrated and bodies desired further intimacy and intensity. Lydia, however, did not like to play second fiddle to anyone in the desirability stakes, even after retiring from dancing. She was top cat (or top pussy, as she liked to be known). She made her point by deliberately knocking over Josh's tumbler and bending over slowly, showing more than ample cleavage in her red outfit and revealing white suspenders as her dress rode up, drawing watching eyes onto her. As she retrieved the fallen tumbler from the floor, she gave Josh's balls a friendly squeeze to ensure that he was suitably distracted. This worked on him. The others continued, oblivious to Lydia, watching the two lovers hungrily kiss each other as hands fondled tight behinds.

"You know the rules," Lydia said on spotting the continuing erotic canoodling and kissing, after returning the tumbler to its place on the table.

The couple stopped immediately, and to prove she was in control, Lydia grabbed Mercedes's dark hair, pulled her over, and slowly kissed her. Mercedes, enjoying another tongue inside her mouth, eagerly reciprocated by placing a hand between Lydia's legs, and in discovering her wetness groped her for longer than needed to the light applause of those seated. Lydia took an elegant bow, breaking off and noting the taste of Gin.

She whispered, "I'm watching you."

The brief eroticism over, Simon caught Stumpy's attention and suggested a chat at the bar. Stumpy understood. Josh thanked everyone for their hospitality as the two rose from their seats, before emptying their glasses. Stumpy's dates stood apart, a little deflated, both unsure what to do next. Lydia waved them on their way sensing that she for the moment was back in full control.

At the bar, Stumpy updated Simon in a hushed tone, giving details of his successful night's work, munching on peanuts from a club saucer. Simon, satisfied with the update, made a call from the bar's private telephone. Once completed he left the bar; the meeting as far as he was concerned now over.

Stumpy grabbed a final handful of nuts and walked off towards the upstairs VIP area, assuming Mercedes and the Vamp were still available for his needs. He still had an itch left over from the earlier evening's dogging show.

They were still free, but not in the same booth after their striking off from Lydia.

David raised himself from his seat and bid Josh a good evening, recommending that Lydia accompany him for the remainder of the night and help him settle, especially since he and Simon had dealt with some business relating to the Rabbi earlier.

Lydia scowled on hearing his name but was secretly delighted to spend the evening with Josh, especially as it was sanctioned. She, being inquisitive, needed to know what made the man tick. Josh thanked David for his hospitality and was equally as happy when Aisha arrived with a second bottle and fresh glasses.

Lydia, having stood like the perfect hostess since showing her face, took a seat opposite Josh and instinctively poured them both a drink. Josh removed a cigarette from its red box.

Lydia, with a definite glint in her soulful eyes, waved a finger, stating, "Not in here, mate. The smoking ban also includes private members clubs."

She removed an e-cigarette from her Hermes handbag and took a lungful of vape exhaling directly into Josh's face, teasing him with her enjoyment of the vanilla flavouring. Lydia had a spare e-cigarette and after further puffs produced it from her handbag and offered it to Josh. He accepted and inhaled the warm vape, blowing it in her direction as expected, before taking a swig from his glass.

"What now?" he asked, changing the subject. He wanted to steer the conversation back towards further sexual engagement. The boss had given permission, after all.

"How about a dance?" Lydia said, winking and gently caressing his leg with hers.

"Thought you retired," Josh responded, cheekily.

"Not me, chicken, the girls."

Josh realised she was playing again, perceiving that she was the jealous type. She continued.

"You looked like a rottweiler in heat with all that salivating when those two sluts were performing thirty minutes ago."

Josh, still fondled by Lydia's Leg, decided to do similar by overtly feeling her inner leg with his hand, enjoying the smoothness of her stockings, saying, "They are good, aren't they? I can still smell them. They radiated sex; can't you smell it? And yes miss, please can I have a dance? And can I keep playing with you?"

Josh would have enjoyed a private dance with the girl couple, but Lydia seemed to be on heat herself, a mixture of scent and sex radiating from every pore. She decided she wanted and required further pleasure. Mercedes and the Vamps show turned her on, but she was not about to let Josh know that. He winked as he proceeded to ease her legs open with his hand and rubbed between them, discovering knickers wet with her love juice. Josh teasingly withdrew his hand, pouring himself a whisky from the fresh bottle, drinking slowly, savouring the flavour before swallowing. Her face told him she wanted extra, but for the second he was in control of the tease.

"I'm off for a smoke; I need real nicotine. See you in ten."

With that he stood up, poured Lydia a whisky, pecked her on the cheek and left.

She, for once, said nothing.

Outside the main club door, Josh took a cigarette out of its box and remembered his Zippo was on the booth table. The door attendant opened the door for him and proffered a light. Josh allowed the attendant to spark up his smoke. Nodding a thank you, he shifted ten yards. He needed time to focus on the business element of the evening.

It still bothered Josh that Rachel plainly knew more and had not said anything; surely her allegiance was to him before her family. Questions were required when back in London: was he of genuine use to the family or were they setting him up to be some sort of fall guy? Again, his wife should know the answer. He could always tell when she lied. He continued smoking with his mind searching for answers, but only thinking of questions.

He dragged on the cigarette to its filter and was about to light a fresh one, when luckily for his lungs and brain, he was interrupted by Lydia who caught him by surprise.

"We still have half a bottle. I don't like drinking alone and I have this for you."

She handed him a brown envelope.

"What's this for, are you paying me for a service?"

"Cheeky bastard. It's your wages, or more precisely, holiday pay. You're a lucky git, getting paid holiday wages before a stroke."

"Oh yeah, tar, didn't realise I got paid in readies."

"Simon wants you to check and then sign here. Every penny is listed and accounted for; the family don't want an Al Capone from the authorities."

Josh did as asked and opened the envelope and counted the new notes.

"An archer - very nice of them."

She looked up at him.

"An archer is two grand - Lydia goes with Geoffrey."

"I see. Can you sign?"

"After a kiss." He pulled Lydia in, and she obliged with a peck on the cheek and nothing else.

"That'll teach you, I'm not that easy," she said laughing handing him a filled in Pepper Wilder receipt book. Josh began to feel the night breeze as he signed and returned the receipt book and followed her back in, again acknowledging the door attendant.

Back at their table he looked around for his lighter. Josh guessed Lydia had likely lifted it. He also knew it would be fun finding it later.

Lydia poured further drinks. Once they were seated, he removed a cowboy boot, nestling a free foot between the warmness of slickly clad thighs, Josh feeling soft warm flesh and her Brazilian shaven pussy as Lydia slid down her knickers, opening her legs allowing further exploration to her growing responsiveness. She drank from her glass greedily, replenishing another for herself and draining the contents. She then poured another, but with a slight tremor as Josh continued to toe inside her vagina in a circular motion. Lydia enjoyed the building sexual energy, knowing a toe alone would not provide the ultimate goal. Her body was gyrating to his toe motion. Eventually, needs took control. Josh sensing this removed his sex sodden digit. Standing up from his chair and using both hands he swung her chair around so she faced him, longing evident in her eyes. Her legs stayed wide as did her soaking pussy, pushing him face down into her wetness, desperate to cum. He obliged but first teased her with his fingers deep within.

"Tongue me out. Eat me now," she demanded in a needy tone.

Josh looked up at her indigent face, removing three fingers.

Lydia pushed him back down.

Josh slid his tongue inside her eager opening, tasting sweet female nectar as he flicked at her clitoris and circled it gently, and bit it to screams of passion.,

She murmured "Harder, go deeper, eat it all, fuck me with your mouth!"

Josh did as she demanded and ate, widening her lips, bringing her to the brim, hands grabbing at the chair legs as she came in waves. He licked as her explosion flowed. Her pussy convulsing in eager satisfaction. Her hands on the chair relaxed as she finished.

Josh stood upright, admiring his mouth work and her Brazilian shaved pussy, for the moment spent, but wide and sticky with its mixture of saliva and cum. Lydia was looking up at Josh touching her wetness before inserting and sucking on a wet finger.

"It's missing an ingredient."

Josh knew she meant his own seed.

Laughing, standing up pulling her dress down,

Lydia reached for his trouser zip and found his hardness.

Josh knew what was coming.

Except he was wrong, as the booth curtain was pulled ajar and in walked Aisha.

Aisha's intuition, experience and sense of smell told her all she needed. She noted the second bottle was practically empty.

"Another bottle Sir? Madam?"

"No thanks, just the bill and car home please."

Lydia could not help herself and muttered whilst grinning, first directing her gaze to Aisha before settling on Josh's face.

"I'm shagged; he's not, but can it be my car please?"

Aisha responded with "Of course, and your bill as usual is covered."

She left the booth after filling both glasses with the bottle's remaining contents, closing the booth off behind her.

The two occupants sat down knowing the car would wait, watching each other intently as they drank. Ten minutes later, they left their cordoned off booth and walked slightly unsteadily down the stairs. Josh spotted the Penguin by the bar, eating peanuts, nodding as their eyes met. David and Simon appeared to be deep in conversation with a dancer who looked crestfallen. Josh was impressed as the venue downstairs was packed out with punters. Most of the poles were busy with dancers on the podiums and a mixed crowd watching. Currency was strewn all around the podiums closest to his view.

Josh could not see Stumpy or his two female companions. He guessed they were in a booth upstairs.

Home James...

Thirty seconds later, the pair was in the confines of the club Mercedes, albeit with a different, but just as courteous, driver.

"Your place or mine?" Josh asked confidently.

"Always yours," purred Lydia.

Lydia was not yet ready to let Josh into her life. He was a long way off being more than just a good lay. Knowing she lived in the next apartment was her secret, and at least for the moment, that part of her personal life and space was out of bounds.

Josh was the one with the unspent itch. His hardness was in a semi-permanent state after licking Lydia out. She tasted sweet and he craved more of her. Lydia cuddled up to Josh in the rear of the luxury Mercedes, enjoying the warmth of the interior and the pink ambient light which surrounded them. Her tight little dress exposed her long legs naturally: as they were crossed, Josh's hand rested on her leg. His eyes rested on her protruding bullet-like nipples. Lydia enjoyed watching the night-lit streets whizz past from the confines of the vehicle. Her hand drifted onto Josh's semi-hardness which instantly grew full with her touch. Josh responded by moving his hand up and down her stocking-clad thigh, he soon found his way between her inner leg as she uncrossed them in anticipation, allowing his fingers to delve further.

An index finger slipped inside her warmth. Lydia stifled a moan as it found her G-spot.

The driver watched her mouth through the car's rear-view mirror. Lydia tried to keep control, her thoughts drifting to Mercedes and that French kiss and grope. It excited her unusually, as for years Lydia had only held contempt towards Mercedes. She was shuddering at the thought as Josh kept working her G-spot, drawing another erotic spasm. Lydia changed mindset, focusing on his member, needing to suck it. At the wrong instant, as she was about to cum, he removed his finger to taste her sex. Lydia unzipped him to encourage his fingers as his stiffness sprang out ready for action. To her surprise Josh deliberately did not return his fingers to her depths, ignoring the encouragement. Instead, he was concentrating on her warm caress of his cock, watching as Lydia's lips pouted their need. Josh, with self-control, removed her hand and zipped himself up. He kissed her hard on the lips and whispered, "Later."

"Hey, Driver," he said simply, "what is your opinion are the merits of Jaguar, BMW and Mercedes as comparable cars?"

The driver, in a Scottish accent, put his view succinctly, from a driver's perspective first. He also pointed out various clubs and bars, highlighting - as he put it - "the pulling joints."

The small talk and jocular conversation had the desired effect on Lydia.

She took Josh's hands in hers and kissed him. The driver observed this through the rear-view mirror. Naturally, she enjoyed this. After all, she was an exhibitionist, who also wanted to regain control in their lustful game. Josh understood her message, especially when she again bit his lip, this time the upper, and as before drew blood.

"Draw," he said, acknowledging her attempts at their game. Lydia fed him an evil stare.

The car pulled up at the entrance of the apartment block. Its driver gave the apartment number to the intercom speaker, the gate lifted, and they drove sedately to the main entrance.

On pulling up, the driver, as a good chauffeur does, was out the car before its occupants had even thought about it. The car door opened, and Lydia stepped out with the driver averting his eyes but seeing just enough of her long slender legs. He was slightly jealous, as he knew the fun Josh was bound to have once within the apartment.

"Shall I wait?" enquired the driver.

"No fanks I can manage m'self," replied Josh with a slight smirk on his face. He took out a crisp tenner from the holiday envelope.

"Driver, 'ere's a cockle for you," Josh said, as he handed the crisp note to the grateful driver. The driver thanked him and promptly returned to the driver's seat of the S-Class.

Bang on the Window...

Josh, on entering the building, found Lydia already at the lift door. The door opened.

"Ladies first."

"If you insist," she replied, stepping into the vacant lift.

Lydia was on him like a cougar before the doors closed. Josh stimulated, grabbed her behind firmly, kissing her full lips before lifting her. Lydia began wrapping her legs around him, their bodies falling onto the lift's cold metal wall. Her legs straddled his body as he frantically unzipped.

The lift doors opened.

They stopped.

A young Deliveroo rider stood, mouth wide open, white safety helmet in one hand, pizza box in the other, at the open lift door. Lydia did not perform for boys. She laughed, trying to look embarrassed whilst untangling from Josh. He took her hand and led her to his apartment front door. They did not look back. The pizza boy did, and he got an eyeful of Lydia's long legs, suspender belt and knickerless arse.

The couple fell into the hallway in concupiscence, and Josh shut the door with his left leg as mutual sexual passion reached boiling point. His tongue hard in her eager mouth, Lydia was devouring it, anxious to explore.

Strong arms lifted her, as legs clung around his torso, the two bodies were in a python like grip. Lustful motion was conveying them to the glazed living room window. Lydia was driven by the coldness of it against her buttocks. The window providing light from the surrounding buildings, Josh unzipped his trousers, forcing himself against her, his cock hard with lustful anticipation. Lydia was reaching for it, desperately guiding its thickness into her slippery, delirious pussy, and Lydia took it deeply, whimpering as it ravaged her core. Josh pumped hard as her vaginal muscles squeezed, encouraging his throbbing build-up.

"Not yet - don't you dare cum till I'm ready!" she commanded. "Bite my tits hard as I cum."

Josh thrust harder as she neared, doing his best to hold back.

Lydia's face expressed, "now!"

He bit her nipples hard.

She screamed "I'm coming! I want yours now."

Josh ejaculated into her, filling her as she came.

For a moment they clung to each other, passionately kissing, gulping oxygen down into their lungs.

Finally, both fell onto the hard wooden floor, exhausted. Sleep came on quickly.

Lydia woke first from the cold mixture of cum between her legs and early morning daylight.

Standing up, pulling her dishevelled dress down over her exposed breasts, nipples erect from the coldness of the apartment, she bent down over Josh who was still asleep and checked the time on his wristwatch. It said 3:45 a.m. The time confirmed, she walked to the bathroom and took a quick hot shower.

Eight minutes later, dressed in a white bathrobe, she was in the kitchen preparing fresh coffee with the bean grinder.

Espresso beans ground, she called Josh.

He woke up in a slight start, for a second not recognising the surroundings and light-headed from the evening's drinking, his cock feeling sore from the last twenty-four hours activity.

"Yeah," he responded slowly getting up.

"Have a quick shower, I can smell my pussy on you," she jokingly said from the kitchen.

Josh now standing answered back with, "Good idea."

He groggily walked into the wet room.

Removing his clothing, he stepped into the water's warmth and soaped himself fully with the coconut shower gel they had played with the day before. The mirror was highlighting deep scratch marks on his back, courtesy of Lydia marking territory. That would take some explaining, he decided, after examining further red claw marks on his chest and buttocks.

Lydia called him as he pressed the off button for the shower. He patted himself down with the white Egyptian bath towel and dressed in the remaining bathrobe hanging from its hook, smiling to himself as he found the missing Zippo lighter. Sliding the wet room door open, he inhaled the freshly brewed coffee and followed its scent.

Two full espresso cups sitting on the glass table greeted him, with a smiling Lydia sitting on the sofa smoking one of his cigarettes.

"Morning," she said jovially.

He sat down next to Lydia without touching her, taking a sip of the warm espresso, it tasting as good as it smelt. Lighting a cigarette from the reappeared Zippo, he filled his lungs and coughed as always with the day's first draw on America's finest tobacco.

"Found it have you?" she said, laughing.

Josh ignored her and decided to push the Joseph question as he smoked.

"Tell me about Joseph."

Lydia looked at him thoughtfully.

"I 'erd somfink at the club, his name was mentioned. He was Max's boy

weren't he?"

She, not quite sure what to say, tugged hard on her own cigarette before stubbing it out in the ashtray.

"Can't tell you," she retorted. "Another coffee?"

With that she got up and made another round while thinking about an answer. Lydia decided that as Max had given instructions to treat Josh as family, giving him a bit of background information would not be an issue.

She sat back down placing fresh filled cups onto the table.

"You have twisted my arm. But what I tell you is between us and these glass walls."

Josh raised his cup in acknowledgment, sat back and waited for another family history lesson. She began, but somewhat coyly.

The family originally came from East London. Max started out as a market trader selling fruit and veg in the Brick Lane area, serving the mostly Jewish community. Josh pulled a face. He hated that word "community". To him it seemed to be used too often. She ignored his expression and continued. Max used to help the weaker and impoverished, who often purchased their weekly shopping from him. He often gave them extra. This led to favours being asked, usually meaning strong-arm tactics on bullies, racists and dodgy slum landlords who increased rents ad hoc in their slum housing, where families shared single rooms and outdoor, unhygienic toilets. Eventually the wealthier Jews from Essex heard about his good deeds and helped him expand his business, lending him money at an exceptionally low interest rate.

Lydia, confident in her knowledge, continued. Max began buying other stalls pitches and renting them out to others. Cutting a long story short, he eventually purchased the whole market (or the land anyway) stopping sales from his stall and collecting rent from the stallholders.

She lit another cigarette from Josh's box and continued. Joseph at this time was now a strapping twenty-something and was using strong-arm tactics himself but was dabbling with the criminal fraternity. He sort of drew Max in; Max obliged and was happy to invest in Joseph's schemes. He, that is Max, liked this quick and easy way of making money.

"I think he liked the danger; he actually began helping his boy out. Drugs were a big opportunity, but only supplied to prostitutes, their pimps, and the odd punter who wanted drugs to help their sexual prowess. This led to dodgy landlords' property being bought at knock-down prices, again in mainly Whitechapel. They were filled with available tenants after building improvements, the less-improved accommodation let out to eager girls willing to work inside rather than up an alley wall with knee-jerkers - an all-round safer environment away from the bully pimps and dodgy punters. Money flowed with the girls keeping a higher percentage of their earnings. Max always made sure the girls were cared for with medical bills and good, safe abortion contacts. They lived in nearby flats, property again acquired and owned by Max, but in a limited property company name."

Josh yawned. It was nearly 4:30 a.m. and his body needed more sleep. Lydia continued, as he made a fresh brew of coffee from the kitchen.

"Joseph was becoming too big-headed and began taking dangerous risks. Max warned him, but to no avail. This eventually attracted the attention of the local police, but more importantly, the local gangland boss. Max, however, formulated a plan, selling off many of his London assets, keeping the newly bought warehouse in Limehouse and moving north into an affluent Jewish area. Joseph, recently married with a young family, continued in his dangerous folly, expanding the drugs business, ignoring the demands of the larger gangster families here in Manchester and down in London, albeit from his new home here in Manchester."

Lydia herself was now feeling the strains of a long day and cut the story even further. Eventually she said, "He was nicked for crimes up here and ended up doing time. It was here in Manchester that he first met..."

Josh interrupted and said, "Yeah, Stumpy. Know that bit."

Lydia took this opportunity and simply said, "Bed."

Josh could see that he would not get anything else out of her, picked her up, and with her arms wrapped around him walked the few mezzanine steps upstairs to the bedroom. The blinds were closed, keeping the early dawn sunlight out. Josh gently put her down on the bed, not seeing that her bathrobe opened as Lydia stretched out, yawned, and mumbled, "Good night."

Josh turned over in his mind what Lydia had told him. It was all remarkably interesting, but still no word on what happened to Joseph. He felt he needed to know. Sleep took hold. Subconsciously, he was not that bothered, for sleep brought with it a rematch with Lydia.

Joseph...

The smell of fresh coffee, as earlier that morning, woke Josh from his deep and satisfying sleep. Lydia was "playing wife". The coffee, sitting in its white espresso cup, was beside him on the glass-topped bedside table. After rubbing his eyes awake, he reached out for the hot black liquid and on taking the first sip realised that Lydia was not beside him, snuggled under the duvet. He, for a brief moment, wondered where she was. Josh smelt the delicious smell of bacon as it wafted up his nostrils. A Yiddisher boy's perfect start to a day, "kosher bacon". He lit his first cigarette of the day, sat back and relaxed, knowing today, Friday, would be spent enjoying the hospitality and body of Lydia.

Bacon eaten and several cups of coffee later, the pair showered and dressed separately. Josh again turned the conversation to Joseph.

Lydia, as before required some gentle prompting. Josh reminded her of where the conversation finished earlier before sleep took control. She again became apprehensive and tried avoiding the subject by playing the good host and instead, offering to pop to the local newsagent as they were low on cigarettes. He did not stop her, and off she went.

Again, unknown to Josh, Lydia returned to her own apartment. She preferred to phone Simon for further advice on the subject of Joseph. In her own mind, it was not a problem, but a confirmation call was necessary. Her insecurities were creeping out, feelings she had suppressed for years were entering her mind. Josh had an unusual effect on her, yes, but worse still was the brief kiss with Mercedes. This scared her; falling for somebody was not in her DNA, especially a female. She occasionally wanted same sex relations, but usually only in a threesome. She could not understand why she fancied Mercedes, especially since she had never fucked her or thought about her in that way before. Mercedes was always the underling that wanted to steal her position. Josh was married and clearly practised extramarital sex. She could focus on suppressing those feelings easily. He was a good fuck and nothing more.

On arrival at her apartment, Lydia first retrieved fresh clothing from her extensive walk-in wardrobe. The clothing was new and still in its original carrier bag, complete with receipt and price tag. The clothing was on the frumpy side, more middle-aged office worker than night-people wear, ideal for the day's deceit. She also added underwear to the bag. They were not frumpy. Two fresh packets of Marlboroughs were collected from a well-stocked kitchen drawer.

Settling down onto her comfortable sofa, she made the all-important phone call to Simon.

Josh was bored: an hour had passed since Lydia had

left. Her mobile went unanswered when he called. Morning TV was not his thing, so he called Rachel instead. She was happy to hear her husband's voice. He brought her up to date, even mentioning the date with religion on Saturday morning. Josh tried the Joseph question on her. Rachel, on hearing her father's name just sobbed, but in between sniffing and crying did say he died in prison, violently. She would not say more. Josh told the truth when he said he was missing her and was looking forward to getting home. Following on from her usual blowing of kisses, he ended the call.

Still unable to contact Lydia, he unpacked his suitcase and hung his clothing up. The wardrobe was full, which naturally surprised him. The clothing and two pairs of shoes were new and in his size. Rachel clearly had input on their purchase. He pondered on when his trip to Manchester was conceived, and by whom.

The intercom broke his thoughts.

"It's me."

Lydia's voice sounded seductive on the intercom. He buzzed her up.

"Shopping? Ah, I only wanted a packet of fags, what've you brought me?"

"No lover, I needed a change of clothes. The local shopping mall is closer than home. Don't mind if I change?"

Lydia did not wait for a reply, smiling wickedly at

Josh as she entered the wet room to change. His eyes followed her as she walked. Turning round, Lydia threw one of the cigarette packets at him which he caught in his right hand.

He removed the wrapping from its box and lit up as he slumped onto the sofa.

He had smoked three from the fresh packet by the time Lydia took a seat beside him. Her appearance created laughter; she was wearing baggy brown army-type trousers and a non-matching yellow wool jumper with a cat design knitted in. The clothing did a good job of hiding her perfect curves.

"Gone 'four by two' wife 'ave you?" he said between laughs.

"No. I don't want you pawing me while I tell you about Joseph," she replied, lighting up a cigarette and blowing smoke into his face.

Josh stopped laughing and responded with "Okay, I'm all ears."

Lydia thought for the moment, trying to remember where the conversation ended previously.

Josh prompted her; he could see she was slightly tongue-tied. He grinned at her and turned to face her on the sofa, taking her left hand into his right. It was soft and silky; Lydia immediately relaxed. Josh was slightly confused as to why she was having such difficulty with the Joseph question: after all, she was a paid employee, not family, and what he was asking was within her remit.

She kissed him on the lips, but not in a desirable way, more of a long-term, wife-like sort of way.

Keeping hold of his hand she began:

"As you know, Joseph's cell neighbour was Stumpy. Stumpy at this time was a fitness fanatic and former bodyguard, more commonly known as a body for hire and sometimes illegal boxer, which, as you know, is the reason why he ended up inside. He was used like a gun for hire, except as a rule Stumpy did not use weapons as his physical presence was usually enough. Again, as I believe you are aware, Joseph was not averse to using his muscle in a similar fashion. Not only were they prison pals, but they were also the only Jews on the wing. Being locked up for up to twenty-three hours a day made them good mates. They soon wangled extra time out of the cell by turning religious. Joseph was at home with this ploy, it was the way he was brought up. He soon managed to get Friday afternoons in winter out of his cell, and most of Saturday off for the Sabbath and, as you know, with all those Jewish Holidays..." She was grinning at this point.

Josh interrupted and said, "It was the Jews that got extras out of the prison system first, before the Muslims."

He laughed aloud as he imagined a bunch of Jewish guys running around prison claiming they were now religious and could not eat pork or bacon, only kosher food and chicken soup.

She put her middle finger to his lips, kissed him on the cheek and continued.

"They used this to their advantage. Other Jews within the prison heard this exploit on the grapevine and followed suit.

"Business soon followed. Jewish prisoners, like everyone else in such places, require difficult-to-find luxuries, and this paid well in tobacco and pills. Tobacco, cannabis etc. were easily smuggled in; the wives with their unsexy clothing and, more specifically, wigs could hide extra allowances of tobacco and illicit soft drugs. These tasks were undertaken by the wives of those who needed to pay back favours, usually protection, which Joseph and Stumpy provided in return. Naturally, protection was only given once payment had been received."

"How?" Josh enquired, in apparent wide-eyed innocence.

"Easy. On leaving, the men would embrace their loved ones, stroke and fondle their lady's hair and retrieve the hidden items."

Josh again smiled, imagining the scene taking place. He retrieved two glass bottles of coke from the fridge as she continued her story, opening the bottles and passing one to Lydia, who stopped mid-conversation and drank thirstily from it. She deliberately allowed some of the coke to spill from her mouth, licking it in a provocative fashion.

She then continued her story as if her light teasing had not taken place.

"The scheme of theirs continued unhindered for nearly two years. All was peaceful on the boys' wing; they had themselves a life of luxury, relatively speaking. They ended up supplying most of the wing with their goods. You could say everyone was happy, even the screws, for they had an easy job. Happy prisoners are quiet prisoners. Some of the screws turned a blind eye, some even helped, for a fee of course. Things began to collapse when inmates from another prison arrived.

"Why were they transferred?" Josh inquired.

"Simple really - the other prison, after a riot, needed a wing refit. Intrinsically the new inmates made themselves busy and began their own business, ignoring the established hierarchy. Feathers and more were ruffled. Business took a downturn for Joseph and his small crew. Accidents began to happen to some of his regulars. Falling over in the showers was the claim from some, others suffered apparent self-inflicted injury in the workshop: fingers or toes lost by clumsy users of equipment. Same problem occurred in the kitchen with carrots missed and fingers chopped.

Josh mentioned the screws.

"Easy," she continued. "They had their own pet screws from their prison who transferred over with them. These screws were always conveniently on duty when accidents happened. The prison reports always stated accidental injury, even if a left-handed prisoner lost a finger or two on his left hand. No enquiry or real interest was taken even by the prison wing governors who signed off after investigation before the main governor confirmed he was happy with efforts made.

Action was taken on Joseph part, or should I say Stumpy. He jumped the gun and made himself "war footing active". His first victim was a young guy who was found strong-arming one of Joseph's couriers. This courier had what one would call an "all points access" around the prison. He would quietly collect the goods after prison visitors had left and move them quickly to the required customers. One of the customers was, unfortunately, the young guy. This was a trap, and the courier is still now in the prison hospital wing eating through a straw."

Josh breathed hard as Lydia continued.

"Suffice to say this was Stumpy's cue - in fact, that was his weapon of choice. The prison grapevine suggested the perpetrator was the prison bitch to Joseph's rival, the cue - or half of it anyway - was found up his young arse. It's safe to say that even now he is now a giver, not a receiver, of prison dalliances. Other rivals fell victim in a less harmful way."

Lydia lit a cigarette and continued in a haze of smoke.

"A meeting was required, and a supposed truce agreed with Joseph and his enemy. It lasted a week. A screw found Joseph dead, hanging from doubled up prison sheets in the laundry area with eyes apparently bulging out of their sockets. Suicide was the official verdict. Stumpy at the time was conveniently with the prison governors explaining his earlier actions.

The prison governor took action before Stumpy had the opportunity for revenge. He was simply moved to a different block with no action taken from the authorities. Naturally, no one heard or saw anything. The other injuries were again put down as accidents."

She continued, wiping a tear from her face. She was not sure why she felt this way because she had never met Joseph. Josh hugged her on spotting the tear and poured her a whisky from a bottle he found in the kitchen.

"Revenge was sanctioned from outside. A new inmate who just luckily happened to know the family contacted Stumpy, who Max became aware of slightly before Joseph's death. He's the Rasta, who runs the family's distribution around the Chapel Street area of Leeds."

Josh looked surprised on this mention. Lydia, noticing his facial expression quickly explained the Rasta.

"He, after proving himself in the prison, is trusted almost as much as me. In fact, you will meet him in the morning before synagogue. He will be the one humming

Bob Marley tunes in dark sunglasses whatever the brightness of the day." Josh had forgotten about that duty and grimaced on that, as Lydia continued.

"His name is Bob, but he's known as The Wailer for obvious reasons.

The rest of what Lydia had to say was straightforward. Joseph's rival lost the power of speech when the Wailer removed his tongue using a borrowed Stanley knife from the prison workshop. This, like before, went down as attempted suicide. Things got worse for him after he left prison on early release on compassionate grounds, as his live-in girlfriend was found dead from a drug overdose. Apparently, her drug of choice, heroin, was too pure and her drug-abused body could not manage such a hit. Her dealer, a Rastafarian-" Josh looked up. "No, it was not the Wailer," she continued. "They had bumped into each other at a rave and he, with some of his pals, invited her back to a squat where she partook in what I was told was a gangbang from other non-involved squat occupants. She, according to Bob, who heard on the grapevine-" Lydia broke off from subject, saying, "See what I did there?"

"Smart arse," responded Josh, as he squeezed her arse hard, saying, "Pray continue."

"The brass was a willing participant and happily indulged in all kinds of erotic games, including BDSM, all for a small bag of heroin and £100 which was found in her handbag. No one was charged, as the squat was a forensic nightmare. There was too much cross-contamination and the fact that she was a prostitute made DNA and semen found inside every orifice impossible to distinguish whose was whose and whether she was willing or not."

Lydia breathed in hard, as the thought of hard cocks inside her was having its usual effect. She finished off her glass of coke and glanced at Josh.

"What's a gangbang, Miss? "

Josh could see that her expression was one of desire; or was it lechery? He was not quite sure.

Lydia smiled wickedly and repositioned herself by jumping on Josh. He responded by pulling her body close to his. He held her face gently, but for only a brief second, before kissing her deeply and passionately, enjoying the sensation of her mouth bringing him to erection. He removed her unsexy top, revealing breasts with nipples as erect as his cock. Lydia felt its hardness beneath her own urgent throbbing, gyrating on its eagerness as Josh toyed with her breasts before encircling her ripe nipples with his mouth, biting and sucking, concentrating on her left.

"Northern girls have two tits, cockney. One's lonely, fucking bite it. Fuck, do it!" Lydia screamed, desperately.

Undoing his fly, as Josh pinched and bit to demand, Lydia was rubbing his tip, enjoying pre-cum trickling onto her fingers. Josh rolled her off as she sucked her fingers, sliding to the floor, pulling off her baggy trousers and parting her black satin panties. Josh positioned himself between her thighs, kissing and licking at her eagerness. She came too quickly for him to continue, her body quivering in after-lust. Lydia despised exploding that fast, but her urgent need was partly driven by an imaginary vision of a drug-fuelled gangbang, and Josh's expertise in carpet-munching - it was just far too powerful. He felt her tense up just before her legs forced him deeper inside as her pussy exploded.

The intercom buzzed as Lydia screamed in lustful ecstasy.

"Fuck" was Josh's reaction to the continued buzzing. His cock needing and expecting her warm mouth.

Lydia, relishing in waves of continual enthusiasm, shouted, "Answer the fucking door."

Josh, knowing he would have to wait, composed himself before standing up, reached up and pushed the intercom using his other hand to wipe her juice off his face.

"Yes," he responded in a somewhat agitated tone.

The intercom responded in a similar tone. The voice was male.

Josh did not so much as recognise the voice, but given the heavy breathing sound of a clearly overweight man, he guessed right.

He pressed the button and responded with "Come on up, Mark."

Mark grunted, entered the building and slowly

wobbled to the lift, giving time for Lydia to dress. She too grunted as she desperately wanted Josh's cock in her mouth and needed another orgasm. One for her was never enough.

The Wailer...

Across Manchester, close to Cheetham Hill, a well-built black man known as the Wailer was also pulling up his trousers.

His expression, unlike Josh's, was one of full contentment.

The Wailer had spent the last three hours with two beautiful women, both also wearing contented expressions, but little else.

The women were entwined around each other on the king-size bed, both watching the Wailer dress. He had his back to them but could see they were fingering each other. He watched intently through the large mirror opposite the bed, making a point of flexing his toned body to their obvious delight. He finished dressing and kissed them both passionately on the lips but reserved full French for Mercedes, knowing her English Rose girlfriend known as the Vamp would be jealous and more enthusiastic next time. He felt she held back, and that was not going to happen again. Next time he would report her to Lydia, and she would have her back working the streets as quick as you could say "Mercedes".

He picked up his car keys from the dusty side table, opened the front door, and left without looking back, hearing joint cries of imminent climax as he closed the door. The Wailer was tempted to help finish them off, but knew appointments had to be kept to time. He stepped out of the small nondescript flat, which was above a grotty off-licence and walked to his car. It sat in a side-street opposite a run-down library. He felt the payment from Simon for services rendered made a change from money; the girls certainly knew how to please, at least most of the time. He enjoyed their intimate erotic dance, especially when Mercedes fucked the Vamp with a strap-on, and he took the Vamp from behind in joint enterprise.

Comfortably seated in his recently purchased blue Citroen, bought solely for preventing the many police stops he used to suffer in the more exciting BMW M-series, he pressed the call button on the car's dashboard and on answering, a voice said, “The usual place, I've got someone I want you to meet.”

He finished the call without muttering a word or questioning who he was to meet, started the engine again from a button on the car’s dashboard and drove sedately into central Manchester. He was thinking briefly about his dead parents and their lifelong struggle in their home deep in the rainforests of St Lucia, where the bad rains and flooding had eventually swept their miserable existence away.

Bob was saved from drowning after being resuscitated, then aged twelve. Alone, he was taken in by, and, after schooling, put to work for his rescuer benefactor, a wealthy Frenchman. At fifteen, after being found in a compromising position with the Frenchman's eldest daughter, he was promptly thrown out.

He discovered a talent for all things illegal and eventually found himself in the UK and prison, where he met his present employers. The reggae sound from his mobile broke his thoughts.

The Penguin Disturbed...

Mark, finally out of the lift, wobbled towards the familiar door. It was opened on his arrival.

"Afternoon, come in," said Josh.

Mark nodded, entered, and immediately spotted the knickers under the glass-topped table. He gave Josh a knowing smile, knowing as usual that this was how Lydia marked her territory. He had seen this from Lydia before. It was also how she, in an unsubtle way, showed that her fun had been interrupted and was likely sulking somewhere.

"No Lydia?" puffed the Penguin.

Josh responded sharply with a hint of humour.

"Nah mate, she's in the bog, playing with 'er favourite fat ten-inch dildo."

The Penguin, hot under the collar from the walk, and slightly embarrassed that Josh likely knew he could not manage a play with the staff pussy, was stumped by the quick response.

Josh noticing his demeanour, grinned and said, "Yeah, there's even a waterproof Rampant Rabbit in the cabinet."

It was not actually in the cabinet. When Lydia popped out to buy cigarettes, he had discovered a collection of adult toys within a mirror cupboard covered by a small number of folded female clothes which Josh assumed were Lydia's. Of course, the Penguin thought he was only joking.

Lydia however was doing just that. She had thought about using the mini rechargeable rabbit from her hidden collection but decided against it. The toy hum would be audible in the next room. She did not want Josh going hard whilst talking business with the Penguin.

"Drink?" offered Josh.

"Whisky, thanks."

"Malt?"

"Yeah, that'll be fine."

Josh stepped into the kitchen and called out to Lydia, "We 'ave a guest."

"Coming," was her response.

She was breathless, after coming the other way.

Josh poured three double pub measures of Black Johnnie Walker into whisky tumblers, making a point of using the ones with the Pepper Wilder emblem. On returning to the living area, he saw that the Penguin was now seated, playing with Josh's Zippo lighter.

He handed the Penguin his drink, placed Lydia's on the table, and took a swig from his own, after clinking Mark's glass.

"I'd lost that," he said, referring to the Zippo, which Josh had again misplaced after retrieving it from the bathrobe.

"I sat on it" was the Penguin's reply.

He felt more at ease, especially after drinking the double, and poured himself another.

Josh took a cigarette from his packet on the table, and on seeing this the Penguin threw him the Zippo. Whilst lighting his smoke, the Penguin pointed out the reason for his unannounced visit. They were to have company. He was to meet the Wailer today, not tomorrow.

After a brief conversation and the reappearance of Lydia, who swiftly disappeared when her mobile rang, Josh decided that the man known as the Wailer would be an interesting character to meet. The two continued with small business talk, with Josh fully understanding the esteem and position that Lydia held within the family.

The Wailer Again…

The wailer stopped the reggae ringtone by answering the phone via the car's Bluetooth system.

"Yeah, man?" he said, before seeing or hearing who the caller was. He was slightly annoyed; two calls in succession whilst reminiscing had disrupted his thoughts.

The voice on the other end brought him straight back to reality. It was the voice of the dead Turk's brother, easily identified by his Pigeon English, unlike the dead sibling. The Wailer's mind raced as he thought quickly. Naturally, he knew of the events in Leeds, but he decided he best play dumb.

"What's up?" he answered in an uninterested tone.

"It's brother, he's been got at. He's dead."

"What? Bro, is you serious? How?"

"Got the lowdown from a brass, she was there; saw him hot up in a car."

The Turk, called Ezra, was born in Istanbul, unlike his deceased brother. He explained the little he knew; the only real fact was his impending visit to Leeds General to identify the body of his brother. Ezra felt the tears well up. He tried to hide this by making a sniffing noise as if stifling a sneeze.

The Wailer ignored Ezra's struggle to act the hard man.

"Let's meet, not on the burner."

The Wailer knew his mobile was clean with its hi-tech extras. The family, his employers had seen to that. He also knew the Turk did not know his true allegiance. To the criminal world, he was just a face to call on for drug moving, prostitutes or random acts of violence.

Ezra agreed to meet: if this were a paid hit, the Wailer would have info. He always did. That is why the Wailer half expected the call. He already knew his instructions should he receive it. The panic call from the Turk had happened sooner than anticipated but, as usual, he was ready.

The family were already moving in on the dead Turk's patch. The wheels were put in motion before his untimely death. The dead young students and the other consequences had just given them an easier in.

"Fifteen minutes. You know the pub on Bury Old Road?" Ezra knew the one. It was where the Wailer liked to hold court.

On finishing the call, the Wailer did a U-turn, and said "Mark" into his hands- free system. The system responded, via its voice recognition software.

The Penguin let his mobile ring, as he was more interested in ogling Lydia. Even a limp-dick could enjoy a highly sexed, attractive female as she reappeared from the bathroom. Josh noticed the Penguin's blatant stare, and that Lydia was wearing a different outfit

"Mark, your phone," he said.

As Lydia took her seat opposite Mark, she crossed and uncrossed her legs in a Sharon Stone-like way, flashing her white knickers. Her stock of secret toys and clothes also included underwear. She, as usual when a man ogled her, responded in her natural way, which was always sexual. She was watching as Mark's pupils widened.

Mark answered his phone just before the answer phone kicked in. He nodded as he spoke. The smart phone screen had told him it was the Wailer.

"Bob's gonna be late, he's got some business. Another drink?" He directed his question to Josh but continued to ogle Lydia. He was a bit disappointed that she was now wearing panties.

"Sure, why not. Lydia, will you do the honours?"

Lydia uncrossed her legs, opening them slightly wider than necessary, stood up and leant over, knowing Mark could not help but peer at her braless bust as she first poured Mark his fresh Malt, then winked at Josh as she replenished his.

On sitting down, she lit a cigarette, inhaled and deliberately blew smoke in Mark's direction.

He coughed and got the hint, focusing on Josh, raising his glass to pudgy lips, his slight tremor spotted by both. This was always Mark's involuntary response to Lydia's cleavage. He always wanted to screw her but knew it would never happen. Even if he had full working equipment, Lydia would never have sex with him. He knew he was a fat, ugly fuck; her position allowed her to pick and choose partners, even if money was involved.

The Meet...

The Wailer arrived at the pub within eight minutes. He circled around the block. He was always careful. All looked safe, parking in a busy car park in a spot closest to the pub's saloon entrance.

Locking the car with the remote key fob, he ambled leisurely through the
saloon door. Mary, the rather plump middle-aged Irish Landlady sighted him immediately.

"Usual, Bob?" she said in her Dublin accent, raising her thick eyebrows as she spoke.

The Wailer watched as she took a Guinness glass from under the bar, set it under the cold Guinness tap and pulled it, watching and salivating as the black liquid flowed agonisingly slowly into the upright glass. Once the glass was three quarters full, Mary, having already served another punter, stopped the flow, allowing the stout to settle.

The Wailer was keeping one eye on his pint and the other on the saloon door. Mary, satisfied reasonable time had passed, topped up his pint.

The Wailer passed her a crisp five pound note as Ezra appeared at his side. Ezra took the precaution of using the main pub entrance. It was a watering hole he used occasionally and this way he could see faces and back up if required.

The Wailer acknowledged him with the usual, "Take a drink with me?"

Ezra responded with a hint of sadness in his tone. "Cheers, bro, just a Coke with ice."

Mary dropped ice into a Coke glass and poured Coke from a glass bottle. The Wailer thought "the bastard wont drink because of his religion but will happily peddle bad drugs". It did not occur to the Wailer that he and his bosses were no better. He collected his change from Mary, took his pint, lifting it to his lips and drinking greedily; the first mouthful was always the smoothest on a cold, fresh pint of Guinness. Ezra nodded his thanks, paid Mary with change and ambled towards a table with two stools and sat placing his Coke on the dark wooded pub table. The Wailer followed, allowing the indiscretion as, after all, Ezra was in mourning; respect on his part was fitting on such an occasion. The pair were eyeing each other across the table, Ezra dabbing his forehead with an unwashed white handkerchief as beads of sweat formed and trickled down towards his dark, ringed eyes. The Wailer terrified him. Their paths had crossed before and he always came out worse, but he knew he had to ask. As the head of his family, it was his duty. He was the only one left, except for his wife and young son. The Wailer was drinking at a steady pace, watching Ezra in his nervous demeanour. He was not the only one. Three clearly religious Jewish men were also observing Ezra. A dreadlocked black man was acceptable, but a Muslim in this particular boozer in the Jewish side of town stood out like a bacon sarnie at a Bar mitzvah.

"What's happening, bro?"

"It's me brother. How dead? You know, yes?" Ezra responded in his broken English.

"Yeah man, I heard he burned. He upset some working pussy."

"Pussy, how you mean?" Ezra was confused. He imagined a cat. He could not see how a cat could have got his brother killed.

"One of my stable told me he wanted a free one, his hands were wild with excitement - except for reaching his wallet.

"A horse saw, and a cat did it, me brother in zoo?"

"No, a stable is me girls, pussy I sell."

"You sell cats?"

Smiling, the Wailer attempted to explain again, gesturing with his hands cupped to his chest before moving them outwards

"Are titties. You mean ladies?" said Ezra, slowly beginning to understand. "He no pay?"

"That's it man. He wanted it free, the girl just lost it - had enough, wasn't gonna put out. It seems to me she acted in self-defence, went a bit too far and panicked. Probably the bad drugs, she had taken bad shit."

The Wailer smirking as he said this, knowing Ezra was aware of his deceased brother's reputation of over-cutting product and supplying the local girls with crap. Ezra fully understood there was nothing else to discuss. He knew when he was beaten. He was expected at the morgue. He wished to see his dead brother, needing him buried as per his religion, but the police had still not given permission. Thinking of his brother in that cold lonely place made him angry. He decided to visit the Mosque's Inman after his brother for religious guidance.

He got up to leave. The Wailer let him.

"May he rest in peace, may he sit with Allah," he said. His face said differently, for it still held its contempt for the man. Ezra nodded, leaving the establishment without looking back.

The wailer caught Mary's eye, smiled, and ordered a final pint of Guinness. Mark could wait until he fixed his Guinness thirst, needing one more to cure it. He drank slowly and relaxed, watching the Jewish men in intense conversation, their voices low, talking in Yiddish, but the constant hand gestures told him the conversation was important. Bob could have sworn he heard Pepper Wilder mentioned, but he dismissed it out of hand. He should have known these men if that were the case. He did not. However, they knew him, they were there under instruction from Max. Max was being careful: he had heard rumours that the Wailer had been overtly flash with money.

The Wailer, pint glass now empty, stood up from his

seat, thanked Mary and politely returned the empty glass, leaving via the saloon door and walking slowly back to his discreetly parked car. He started the engine and left the car park, driving carefully to his meeting with Mark.

Meanwhile, one of the religious-attired men telephoned Max from the old-fashioned pub payphone and informed him that Bob had carried out his duties as expected.

Old Buddies & a Hot Penguin...

The Wailer parked his car in the apartment car park, entered the building, keying in the key code and unlocking the entry system key. Ignoring the blank stare of the concierge, he waited for the lift's arrival. He stepped out of the lift on the correct floor and swaggered towards the door he knew so well. The door opened. Lydia was behind it.

"Ha, Bob, haven't seen you since..." she stopped mid-sentence. The occupants behind her did not know they were occasional fuck buddies, usually when she fancied a bit of Caribbean company. Bob was not that well-endowed, but certainly knew how to use it.

Bob hid his surprise on seeing his sometime fuck-partner. She put a finger to her lips.

He understood responding with, "Hah, sis. Like the skirt." He refrained from mentioning her cleavage and somewhat erect nipples under her top.

Kissing her lightly on the left cheek, he gave her arse a sly squeeze. She stifled a giggle, kissed his right cheek, and said, "Mark's here with a guest."

Mark struggled to stand up, his bulk and whisky a hindrance.

"Bob, this is Josh, my brother-in-law. He's our new London end."

Josh stood and shook the Wailers hand, noting his

huge bulk. He also wondered what had happened to the old London end.

"'Ello mate, 'erd good fings about you."

"Yeah bro, nice one."

Bob knew nothing of this cockney, except that he was probably fucking Lydia. It was his eyes: they showed contentment and slight anger (as Mark had likely interrupted them). He also knew that for the time being the apartment and Lydia would be unavailable to him. Lydia handed him a whisky, lit a cigarette, and edged to the kitchen so the boys could have their chat. Bob held her glaze just a little too long. Josh's glare told him they were definitely screwing. A pleasure not for him until the Londoner left.

Mark sensing some slight animosity, broke the silence.

"How are the streets, now the Turk's gone?"

"Yeah, man. No pussy or clubbers have died since the Turk. That whore did a good job."

Mark appreciated the Wailer's tact, believing the fewer people knew the better. As far as he was concerned, besides himself, Max, Stumpy, the Wailer, and the friendly madam were all who knew. He wanted it to stay that way. Even David and Simon were not aware.

"Down to business," he said, as the smell of freshly brewed coffee mixed with cigarette smoke wafted into where the three were sitting.

"Yeah man, present for you." The Wailer handed Mark a brown envelope. It clearly held money. Mark was somewhat surprised, but secretly pleased. It meant that the Wailer was on the level.

"I had some luck; you know what I mean?"

Mark did not need to ask where it had come from, but it confirmed the rumour that he had a score and was sharing it. The wailer was just a little slow in sharing.

Josh observed but felt it best to stay schtum.

Lydia re-entered the living area, three pairs of eyes following as she moved elegantly, placing a hot coffee pot and four white coffee cups onto the crowded table. She collected the whisky bottle and empty glasses, disappearing back into the kitchen, wiggling her pert arse as if it were a wink to all three gentlemen. The Wailer and Josh eyed Mark, who again was hot and bothered having avidly watched another brief performance from Lydia. Mark tried to deflect the obvious by pressing the coffee pot plunger into the glass pot, but all he managed was to produce an explosion of coffee using too much force with the plunger. The hot liquid naturally finding its way over his trousers.

"It's come!" was Josh's comment.

Bob laughed. Mark looked hotter, showing embarrassment, especially as Lydia reappeared with kitchen roll and patted down Mark's trousers. The outcome was further laughter and embarrassment with an increasingly teenage scene until Mark took over the patting down and spoke in an assertive tone.

"Now, Josh, you are expected at Shul Saturday morning with your prayer book and manners - no business talk until after the service. Bob will be on the door as added Saturday morning security, working with the young Jewish men who would rather be there than pray. Bob will be taking business orders for the week ahead from whoever has a need. In this guise, he is agency staff and should be treated as such."

Josh, listening intently understood and stored all the information, including that the agency was another family business enterprise. What he did not expect was a visit to a Jewish old people's home for lunch, a duty Max liked all to participate in. This happened in a rota system with two members of the family visiting each Sabbath day. Josh would attend with Simon and eat lunch with the old folk. It was also explained to him that the home was a clever outlet for disposal of unwanted guests.

"The home," continued Mark, "is a quiet enterprise belonging to Gary. Basically, this means we have some old folk who live on the premises in name and room only. They even have a nurse attend to them - i.e., they visit their room and make busy as if someone exists. Max has friends who are paid to sit in the communal areas who to all and sundry appear to suffer from Alzheimer's or other ailments. Consequently, the real resident old folk leave them alone and the nurse attends to them as if they were real guests, Now suppose a guest needs to disappear," Mark raised his voice and continued with, "it's, simple really. Josh, you remember the elderly Rabbi at Pepper Wilder? He contacts the local quack who issues a death certificate without checking on the fresh corpse, happy to rely on the nurse's expertise. A death in an old people's home is considered normal and post- mortems are rarely required, especially under a doctor. The Rabbi even spends the night with the corpse, as is the custom, and sometimes Max will attend so the Rabbi can have a break. It keeps nosey fossils away. The corpse is later transferred to the cemetery in its coffin, so no one sees it - we even have a few mourners attend the recently deceased. The only drawback is that non-Jews are buried in a Jewish cemetery, but hell, they're dead - who cares? There is some finer detail, but do not concern yourself with that. I can see pussy is on your mind."

Josh almost jumped up from his seat at that comment, for at that second, he was listening intently to the Penguin, but his eyes were somewhat transfixed on Lydia in a trance-like state. All laughed, especially the Wailer, who was actually doing the same but in his usual sly way. Mark decided that the sexual chemistry in the apartment was giving rise to jealously. His wife had long ago given up on trying to get him up, preferring to eat than fuck anyway - a perfect relationship you might say.

Mark stood up, giving the impression he wanted a word with the Wailer about Saturday's business. The Wailer took the hint. Hands were shaken all round.

Lydia and Josh were now finally alone.

Finally, Some Head...

"What's a blowjob, miss?" Josh decided a blatant question was required. He had missed out on head twice now, and he was positive Lydia was equally gagging to do so.

Lydia sat beside him looked thoughtful and gleeful at the same time. She urgently wanted his cock inside her mouth but was going to tease first.

"Well, it's when a person enjoys another's sexual organ with their mouth, but first you want it nice and hard."

Power and control were partly her reasons for giving him head, but as a sexual adventurer who intimately owned and understood her body's need first, she suffered no sexual qualms or guilt about giving.

"Make me hard, Miss."

Josh said this as her hand was already discovering that he was.

Lydia played with his shaft without unzipping, teasing it gently.

"What do you want me to do with your zip Josh? You don't want it unzipped do you?"

"Er, what do you fink?"

"Talk dirty to me first. How much do you want me to suck you?"

"Fucking slut. I want to fill your mouth with my

cum. I want to come over your tits." Lydia slid his zipper down releasing his stiff cock. "And," he said, "I want to watch you swallow the Wailers cock as I fuck and fill your cunt."

"More" Lydia said, his filthy words having an added effect on her vulva.

"Fucking whore, I know you want big cocks in all your holes, spurting cum at once, filling your pussy and mouth."

Lydia put a finger to his lips before their mouths locked, stroking his tongue with her own in imitation of oral sex, focusing on its end. Lydia was removing her top, revealing braless breasts, cupping his balls squeezing gently, kissing, and exploring his wet mouth, feeling its urgency. She responded in gulping hard on his tongue, breathing warmth into his mouth, eyes open watching.

Lydia copied Josh's earlier method and slid onto the floor, kneeling between wide legs, admiring his shaft's girth. Her legs were now wide, like his pupils focusing on the excitement displayed on her panties.

Lydia continued to tease, fingering within her damp knickers with one hand, manipulating his cock with the other. She was feeling its excitement with her consistent spreading wetness.

He did as was expected and desired, pushing her head down on his hardness, her mouth eager for its gift, taking it in, appreciating its length as it filled and stretched. She was gagging on its size, withdrawing, gently licking her way up and down inch by inch to its shaft and opening. One of her hands was rubbing his balls, her tongue concentrating on the head. Licking hard at his dribbling pre-cum, blowing gently, her other hand was working slowly up and down its length feeling impending urgency, switching to what Lydia called ice cream mode, as strong hands forced her down. Taking it all in, switching both hands to his balls. Allowing her mouth to fully appreciate his size as he stabbed deeper into her. She knew he was nearly there, as his cock spasmed and jerked, fucking deep into her throat, Lydia swallowed his seed.

She relished the taste of cum and like everything sexual with Lydia one load was never enough. Focusing on his eyes, their begging wanting more. She obliged by sucking further. Josh slamming back into her with added force, Lydia re-engaged ice cream mode. His pulsating thick shaft was forcing her to gag as her throat filled with cum. She withdrew, this time only swallowing part of his load. Lydia's eyes stayed fixed on his as she swirled cum inside her mouth, mixing it with saliva. Remembering his earlier words, she tongued the mixture out, rubbing the warm fluid into her breasts with two fingers keeping her eyes fixed. His gaze said more. Her pussy said more.

She obliged it and him. Fingers were parting her panties, working her pussy into a frenzy, watching him wank as she fingered.

"Stop wanking, slam it into my throat. I want more of your cum in me."

Josh rammed it in, exploding as demanded as Lydia came onto her fingers.

Be Careful in Tunnels...

Six weeks earlier, in Limehouse, London, Harry Caine, a middle-aged, budding, but not so bright entrepreneur left his workplace feeling good. The warm, bulging envelope in his breast pocket was the reason, for he had had his largest result since he began employment at the run-down warehouse. He was driving to his long-term girlfriend's home to celebrate his good fortune. She, of course, was not aware of how the envelope had ended up in his pocket. To her it was just a bonus, but larger than normal. In Harry's mind, treating her to his good fortune was a way of justifying his deed and ill-gotten gains, and perhaps helping towards her organising a swingers' party, as promised. His plan worked a dream; through his planning and efficiency, it was easy, even though he had somewhat stumbled upon it.

As far as Harry was concerned, the Jews that ran the warehouse were poor employers who only paid the minimum wage. His job as a courier was to deliver stock from the warehouse in the company Ford Transit to kosher restaurants and delicatessens usually around Stamford Hill or Hendon. Harry discovered the drugs after dropping and smashing a crate of kosher wine and, following his initial panic of lost wages, had spotted dark condoms, some split on the hard floor containing drugs - cocaine to be more precise. He soon worked out that certain containers held different markings and that these crates contained the concealed extras, sometimes wine, otherwise concealed in kosher bakery products, but always delivered to the same four names, and often different premises. He decided to follow one of these crates on a day off, following another company courier to its destination. The transit was unloaded at the back entrance as was usual. Some crates, however, were not stacked in the stockroom, but left by the front either by car or motorcycle courier, albeit in much smaller packages. He had made a note of the car that took the largest load and followed it to its final destination. The clever bit, as far as he was concerned, was doing this several times and seeing that the car, always a blue Vauxhall Estate, took a different route to the same destination but always ended up delivering to the same hand.

He, unfortunately, was not intelligent enough to spot that the estate car always had a moped following its journey, and he had been pinpointed on his second tailing. His details were noted and subsequently passed up the chain. The orders initially given were to observe as no one was sure if he was old bill, or a rival trying their luck.

His own car was discovered, registered in his girlfriend's name: one Elizabeth Jane Moore, Liz to her friends or Easy Liz by lesser acquaintances. A family associate on instruction from the family had easily picked her up on her weekly girls' night out. She was shagged senselessly first in the female toilets and again after a cheap meal. Her later bedroom talk was very enlightening on where her partner worked, and that he often could not get it up without the help of sexual aids. Apparently, Harry liked to watch her give fellatio on a dildo before he could perform.

It was decided he would be monitored to see what he did with the family's product before any action was taken.

Harry, who crossed himself whilst thinking of his proudest business moment, pictured the details of his plan. Once satisfied with the car's route and contents, he set up a three-car collision with one of his Polish drinking friends, who often boasted about his insurance scams when drunk. Harry was astute enough not to share the reason why it had to be this particular vehicle, giving the impression that he had been cuckolded by his girlfriend and wanted revenge. The Pole, known to some as Insurance Pete was one of the girlfriend's one-night conquests so did not press Harry for too many details, especially as the pay was above his average for similar work.

The accident occurred at a T-junction on a busy road known as an accident black spot. The estate car had simply collided into the back of a box van, which had braked suddenly for no apparent reason. A car driven by his good self had gone into the back of the estate car at a deliberate low speed, causing only a minor crack on the plastic bumper. The disgruntled driver, after seeing that his car's rear was undamaged, moved to the box van to have it out with the driver who had caused the accident. The box van driver, in his believably broken English, kept insisting a dog had run out in front of him, spending time looking for it with the help of the aggrieved estate car driver. This took some time to communicate to the victim, allowing Harry to retrieve a cigarette from his vehicle, with enough time to move the goods from the estate car to his own - easy when a car is left unlocked, as anticipated during a minor collision. The estate driver and Polish Pete discussed exchanging insurance details with both becoming heated in vocabulary. Harry, at this juncture, returned to smoking and offered to mediate, suggesting cash be paid to the aggrieved van driver, as the estate car was obviously driving too close and should have managed to stop when the van braked, and clearly had not and was therefore the miscreant in the eyes of the law. The estate driver accepted, knowing time and the mention of the word police was a risk he could not take. A small crowd of onlookers had gathered, making him nervous, and helped decide cash to the Polish driver was best suited all round.

Again, unfortunately for Harry, the car driver took photos of the box van's damage and registration plate where he was standing, negotiating a cash settlement.

Eventually the incident was happily resolved with

Polish Pete accepting £250 and all went on their way under the watchful eye of the discrete moped rider.

Harry drove on to his buyer with the goods stashed in his car, focussed on how clever he was and how to spend his ill-gotten gains. He was not aware that yet another car, a Smart, was now tailing him.

Later that evening, Harry, again at the wheel, thought of Liz as he drove into the Lime House Link tunnel, squinting his eyes and focusing on the change of light. His weak eyes did not see the motorcycle tailing him, a Suzuki Bandit with a pillion, pulled alongside his car in the outer lane. On the second bend the rider checked his mirrors, giving thumbs up to his pillion who immediately drew a 9mm semi-automatic Smith and Wesson from his black leather jacket and shot out the front nearside tyre of Harry's car with the second shot. It disintegrated on impact. Harry did not hear the crack of the handgun but saw the flash and heard the revving of the motorcycle engine as its rider dropped to a lower gear and sped off. Harry did feel the effects of a sudden blowout and tried in vain to control his car. His mind, for the second it was still alive, raced as the car fought against his valiant efforts.

The car won and rammed itself into the outer crash barrier before bouncing into the barrier on the other carriageway. Harry battled with the wheel to no avail. The car gave a final push, somersaulted between the barriers, and tore its front end into a different shape. Harry, not wearing a seatbelt, as was his habit, felt the g-force as his body hurled through the windscreen, which cracked under the force of his body weight. Harry felt only a sharp stab of pain as he rolled onto the tarmac, the car crushing his head on its final somersault. The car stopped as his heart did, his brain having spread itself onto the tarmac in a jelly-like mess. Luckily for everyone else, traffic at this time was light, preventing his unfortunate end creating further mayhem.

The motorcycle rider made a phone call once out of the tunnel and pulled into the first side street. The pillion removed the false registration plate, revealing its true identity, and they dropped the gun after smashing it into three pieces with a hammer retrieved from the motorcycle courier box. Two parts ended up in the nearby drain and the other thrown into a nearby communal apartment block refuse bin.

Easy Liz...

Liz was busy dressing and sipping her second glass of cheap Prosecco, pondering on how to split from Harry, her boyfriend of six months, her mind made up after yet another one-night sex session with the handsome stranger she had met during last week's girls' night out. The man performed all night, bringing her to orgasm several times. Later, during after-sex talk, it appeared that he was a member of an exclusive sex club and fan of erotic toys. Liz did not object to playing with sex toys independently or with a partner - or indeed several partners at once. Just not all the time to get a man up. She had suggested to Harry as much, but he could not afford the membership fee despite several promises.

Pouring herself another glass from the nearly empty bottle while reading her copy of Jessica Drake's *Guide to Wicked Sex*, the doorbell rang. She was expecting Harry and was ready to terminate their relationship on the easy grounds of his continued lateness. On answering the door, standing slightly back on opening, there were two police constables, one a young redheaded on her first death duty call.

"Evening madam. Are you Elizabeth Jane Moore and the owner of car registration ANP..."

The young WPC stuttered as she dropped her notebook onto the ground.

Liz nodded, “Err yes, yes. What's wrong? Is it my father?”

“No madam. Can we come in? I think it's better if you sit down.” Responded the experienced officer, observing her body language and smelling the alcohol on her breath.

Nervously and reluctantly, Liz invited them in, shutting her front door.

Aftermath...

Traffic was still chaotic in the Limehouse area, with the Limehouse Link tunnel shut, the barrier down and "XXX" displaying on the overhead screen.

Inside the tunnel, forensics officers were busy at work. Harry's remains, as death was easily confirmed, were on their way to the morgue, his identity established as his driving licence was found in his back trouser pocket in his blood-soaked plastic wallet. A police check revealed the vehicle's owner. Two local police constables were dispatched to the owner's address. It appeared to be an open-and-shut case: the front tyre had blown out, with the force removing it from its wheel and the driver simply losing control, unable to do anything to prevent his demise.

The scene was videoed after the placement of yellow markers accentuating bits of car debris and brain matter, the CCTV footage collected from the central control room to be inspected later. What the forensic team could not find was the spent bullet lodged in the remains of the alloy wheel which in turn was impaled on the car's wheel arch. The first motorist on the scene was chatting to a police officer about what he witnessed.

Prayer Time...

Saturday morning arrived too soon for the new fuckbuddies who were still curled around each other in a spooning embrace as two mobile phone alarms went off simultaneously, creating a cocktail of R&B and an ’80s classic hit. The bedside table digital clock read 06:00. Josh stirred first by shutting off his mobile and throwing it across the bedroom. Using the help of the red glare from the clock he managed to find the other annoying device.

Lydia's alarm lit up on being turned off. It displayed in large lettering, “DROP THAT COCK AND GET UP”.

Josh sniggered to himself as he kissed and nibbled Lydia gently on the back. She stretched but did not stir. Biting her slightly too hard on her left ear achieved success, but not the way he envisioned as she leapt from the bed grabbing the blue quilt, wrapping it around her slender naked body.

“No time to play, lover, we have work to do.”

“What do you mean? My cock wasn't in your mouth,” was Josh's comical response.

“Very funny. You saw my phone then. No wonder I didn't hear its alarm.”

“We, or should I say you, have synagogue today once you’re gone, I’m having a soak and then clothes shopping. I need a new outfit or three.”

Josh, compos mentis, feeling the sudden cold from

the quilt removal and remembering Max's wishes, sighed, begrudgingly stretched and eased out of the comfortable bed, throwing a pillow in Lydia's direction but missing completely. She squealed obscenities at him as he drifted into the bathroom for a hot shower. Lydia, clad in the blue quilt, removed Josh's suit from its place in the wardrobe, retrieving a bathrobe from the floor. She stepped down the few steps to the kitchen, first playfully hiding Josh's Zippo, which she retrieved from his suit pocket.

Josh showered, put on his blue checked three-piece suit, joined Lydia in the kitchen and prepared the espresso maker as she cooked boiled eggs and crumpets. They both tucked in, sitting on stalls beside a small breakfast table.

"I have a present for you," she said, handing an unwrapped hat box over after retrieving it from a small cupboard.

"Just what I've always wanted, a tit for tat. What's that for?"

"It's for your head and the walk to the synagogue," she responded in a dirty laugh and continued, "Put it on, let's see if it makes you handsome."

"No chance."

"It will be worth your while later, promise".

Josh, beaten, stood up and placed the offending item on his head. Lydia watched, laughing.

"Never had a religious man in a fedora before. Can you wear the hat later? You will get more of this," she said erotically, opening her bathrobe and allowing Josh a full frontal of her currently unavailable neatly trimmed beaver.

Josh tried for a grope, unsuccessfully. Lydia stepped back and teasingly said, "Only good boys get to fiddle. Maybe if you eat all your greens later you can help me out and nosh me for afters." She made her point by stroking her mound. "No, not on the Sabbath - especially a sex-hungry shiksa. What will the rabbi think?"

Josh knew she had won, and could only respond, with "Prefer a pork pie topper, me."

Sitting back down, Josh drank the last of the coffee. The intercom buzzed.

Lydia answered it.

"Hey Stumpy, Josh will be down in five."

"Okay Lydia, ta."

Fifteen minutes later, after some further outlandish teasing on Lydia's part Josh was sat in the front passenger seat of the now familiar Volvo and helped himself to a cigarette from Stumpy's packet, which was in its familiar place.

"Good Sabbath," were his first words to Stumpy.

"Nice hat - looks new. Was it a gift already? And good sabbath to you, Sir," Stumpy replied as the Volvo struggled into life.

The journey took only ten minutes as the traffic was still light. Josh was a bit confused as Stumpy stopped and parked the Volvo just off the Middleton Road as he could not see a Synagogue but could see many men of different ages: he presumed old-time gangsters as they were all dressed the same - in fact, the same getup Stumpy was wearing.

Stumpy, giving him a look said, "You have legs, don't you? Nice Yiddisher boys walk to Shul."

Josh had completely forgotten this and replied, "Yeah mate, can't work or ride pussy, it's the Sabbath."

He noted that on stepping out of the car, Stumpy placed his car and house keys into a magnetic box which was attached to the chassis.

"Surprised that works with all that rust and filler."

Stumpy gave him a glare and began to walk back on to Middleton Road. Josh followed whilst lighting a cigarette from a Pepper Wilder matchbox, as his lighter was not in his pocket as it should have been, following Stumpy like a naughty schoolboy. As they neared the top of the road, he noticed the building on the corner of the next junction. It was of 1960s design and plain in its shape. It hardly looked like a synagogue and was set back from the road. The name on the board was the first clue that it was a religious building. It simply said "Mead Hill Orthodox Shul" with the Rabbi's name underneath. He also noticed several younger men at the door huddled around the main entrance in fashionable suits.

Josh was a little confused as it was a different

building to the one Lydia had shown him the other day.

"Good Shabbos," the men offered as they walked up to the building's front entrance. Stumpy and Josh responded with polite nods, the required Jewish response to door staff. Josh had already clocked Bob alone in the car park smoking a joint. They had both ignored each other which he assumed was the right protocol.

As they passed into the main hub of the Synagogue, they were handed the requisite prayer books. Josh followed to the front where they took their seats after acknowledging Max and the rest of the males in the family. On sitting down, he opened his prayer book the wrong way round at first and found the correct page after checking the page number to which Stumpy had turned.

He took in his surroundings, first seeing the Rabbi when he was forced to raise his voice as the congregation became overly loud, no doubt discussing business rather than following the service. The interior was like the outside - boring to say the least. He always thought churches were much classier buildings to pray in. When he was younger, he had wished he were Christian, especially after he had attended his first couple of funerals in his twenties. He felt Jewish burial grounds were cold and devoid of anything other than death, whilst other places of rest at least had a warm calm about them. He also took in the memorial name plates around the raised wooden platform known as the Bimah where the Torahs were kept in their sanctuary. Most of the names seemed to be Cohen or Goldstein, but he did spot Max's family name in memory of Joseph, with this being the largest plaque. The curtains began to open where the Torah was housed. The man beside him struggled to his feet, as did Stumpy - in fact, all did - he somewhat sheepishly followed.

The Rabbi continued on and the men all around him grunted and muttered at the same point; Josh followed. What he did not do was pray, or Duvan as his people called it. The men swayed back and forth bending their knees; Josh held back a snigger. Josh, feeling twelve again remembered the whisky after the service and the slap he received from his father after downing too many glasses and puking up over the Synagogue Shamus whilst they chatted about his pending Bar mitzvah. He also noticed the upper level of the building. Here the women were seated, most in hats, clearly chatting even more blatantly than the men. One was even checking her makeup with a vanity mirror. Josh could not see why as she was pig ugly or, as this was not a kosher expression, a right fat ugly cow.

The service continued and after another prayer session he slipped out and made his way to the empty car park as instructed by the young men on the door.

He soon found the Wailer skulking in a corner, looking depressed.

"What's up mate, not getting enough?"

"Wish dat was the problem. It's de opposite. Me

cock's got me in trouble, I've got a brat baking. It's due in seven months."

"Oh," was Josh's response, his face holding a smirk.

"It's me ex-bitch - she will demand money for it. I'm doing that already with me other old bitch pussy."

Josh was at a loss and said the first thing that sprung into mind.

"Got any gear, mate?"

"Yeah man. I've got coke, Es, smack- whatever you'se want."

"Charley be good, mate – will 'elp keep it up tonight, planning on indulging.

"Lydia," said the Wailer, thinking of what he was missing.

"Maybe," said Josh.

The Wailer retrieved a small clear bag from his trouser pocket and handed it to Josh.

Josh instantly reached for his wallet from inside his jacket pocket as the Wailer said, "You're alright. You're family - it's on me."

"Nice one mate, I won't forget. Best go in. I'm supposed to be playing nice Jewish boy."

The Wailer let him go and carried on thinking about his forthcoming problem. He also needed to do an inventory of his stock which was housed under bramble bushes at the other end of the car park. He expected a little business after the service from the youngsters with too much money and equally high testosterone levels.

Josh returned to the building and realised perhaps he had spent too much time outside. The Sabbath service had finished and the great and the good were thronging around a separate area of the building on his left, through a partitioned doorway. Josh did the expected thing and wandered in. He looked at all the faces; none registered. He helped himself to a shot of whiskey, drank quickly and pulled an unnatural face as it was of poor quality. He actually struggled to keep it down. He placed the equally cheap shot glass down on a silver tray, feeling out of place as the throng seemed unfriendly and only interested in the now untidy spread on the cluttered white paper tablecloth darkened by spilt food and drink. He started to edge back out of the room and felt a tap on his right arm.

"Hello," the owner of the arm said.

Josh turned facing the voice and was somewhat relieved when he realised it was David.

"Good Shabbos," was his response and he automatically offered his hand which David shook firmly.

After a brief chat about the likeness of pigeons and the congregation around their respective food, the pair left the synagogue with David reminding the Rabbi he would see him later that afternoon. Josh followed David, passing Stumpy's Volvo. Three cars further up a Jaguar's alarm system was deactivated by David. On opening the driver's door, he suggested Josh do likewise.

He did not need asking twice.

The engine purred into life as Josh's mobile vibrated inside his jacket pocket. He retrieved it tapped the screen and read, “Be good at lunch and maybe this will be dessert.” Attached to the message was a screenshot of a wide-legged Lydia, wearing nothing but a smile. It ended with “See you at Pepper Wilder.”

Josh tapped in “Only if you taste sweet,” and pressed the send icon.

David noticed and assumed the text was from Rachel.

“Hope you sent her my love.”

Josh nodded. Lydia’s text reminded him of where they were now driving towards.

Lunch...

The Jewish old people were literally around the corner. David swung the Jag into the car park which was protected by a hump barrier which lowered itself when he keyed the pass number into the keypad by the barrier. It was somewhat damaged and bent at a slight right angle, with most of its white paint chipped where no doubt elderly drivers had caught it on entering the premises.

"Welcome to hell", uttered David. His first words since they had got into the Jag, he continued and said "Just do as I do - you may even enjoy the lunch. I may even find you a Girlfriend. I'll make sure she has her own teeth and is under eighty!"

Josh pulled a helpless expression and did not react to David's poor attempt at humour.

In fact, words were not spoken as they left the Jag. David had parked it in a disabled bay and produced a disabled badge from the sun visor, placing it face up on the dashboard.

The home, with its name board attached to the wall by the intercom read "Gan den", as some letters appeared to be missing. David, as before, pressed six numbers into the keypad. The door buzzed and Josh followed David in, passing brass plaques on his left. As in the synagogue, the family name was more prominent than the other names listed. His nostrils also smelt a mixture of urine and bleach. They walked into an open-plan, carpeted hallway, passing a couple of comfortable easy chairs by the front door and straight into a communal area which was filled with more easy chairs, wheelchairs and tables with old people seated on many. Josh was in a fit of the giggles as most residents appeared dead, until one of his imaginary corpses mumbled in a slurred way.

"Daddy, where have you been, where's mummy?"

David patted the elderly head and said, "She's coming."

"You're not Daddy, he is. I want him." The very old lady wagged a bony finger in Josh's direction in an angry frustrated way, and said "Daddy, my Daddy."

Josh, on David's stare, walked towards the Alzheimer's-stricken resident. He breathed through his mouth as the lady smelt of piss, offering a hand in his usual friendly manner. The old lady gripped it with a strength which took Josh by surprise as she pulled him closer, shouting, "Daddy can I have my pocket money? You promised extra so I can buy my doll."

Josh decided he had little choice, and reaching into his trouser pocket, fumbling around for some change, grabbed a mixture of £1 and £2 coins, and handed it to the now smiling lady, who was still holding his hand in her bony grip. Placing her glasses on her face, which were attached to a thick silver chain around her skinny neck, she inspected the money. Throwing the coins at the wall waking the sleeping gentleman next to her, she exclaimed, "I don't want toy money! I want sixpences."

Thankfully at this point, she let go of Josh's hand as an attractive thirty-something Thai nurse intervened.

"Come on Debra, it's lunchtime."

The old lady was certainly agile, as she almost jumped up from her seat and followed the nurse into another room, having seemingly already forgotten about daddy and pocket money. Josh breathed a sigh of relief as she left and noticed the Rabbi from Pepper Wilder - the one known as Octopus - entering from the main door.

He retrieved one of Lydia's e-cigarettes from his inside jacket pocket and inhaled the sweet-tasting vapour.

David said nothing of the incident, as if it were a normal occurrence, and on

noticing the Rabbi, started to chat to the now awake gentleman who wanted to know when it was his turn for lunch. Thankfully, this man, Mr. Sofa, was firing on all cylinders and spoke with a strong German accent. All three had an interesting discussion about pre-war Germany, the man's escape before the war and his long army career, which included the newly formed SAS. The Rabbi joined the conversation but had a problem with eye contact, as his focus kept wandering onto the behinds and cleavages of the attractive nurses who were attending to the needs of the elderly residents.

"Lunch, Mr. Sofa. Do you need a toilet?"

The Thai nurse returned unnoticed by all except Mr. Sofa, as the three visitors were hanging on to his every word, especially the bit about his time in London where he was apparently involved with Jack Spot in the 1950s in London's Soho and held off a takeover bid by up-and-coming East End gangsters that controlled East London.

Mr. Sofa looked up at the Thai Nurse, winked at her and cheekily said "If I was twenty-five years younger I would have had you the moment your beautiful eyes looked into mine."

"Now, now, Mr Sofa: I told you before I'm married and am a good girl." Smiling at the compliment, the thought of Mr. Sofa as a young fit man made her shiver, as she knew she would have let him.

Josh helped Mr. Sofa up from his seat and all followed the nurse into the large dining room, admiring her legs and arse as they went. David and Josh sat down with Mr. Sofa, as both were happy to hear more stories, whilst the Rabbi wandered off to pester more staff members with anything other than religious duties. The occupants were served chicken soup first - or Jewish medicine as it is commonly known - and bread challah, which as usual Josh found rather sweet. The chicken soup reminded him of his mother's as it was too watery and devoid of any flavour, but he did find some real chicken pieces. David continued the conversation with Mr. Sofa, who drank and chewed noisily having difficulty with his false teeth.

The main course, surprisingly, was better. It was chicken and new potatoes, washed down with a glass of kosher white wine which was also better quality than the usual kosher rubbish.

A slight kerfuffle to the right of them broke their continued conversation as a very elderly lady was remonstrating with a young male staff member. Josh strained his ears to hear.

"Stop it! I want the bones there's meat on it."

"You can't! You don't have any teeth left so let me cut it for you."

"No, it's mine leave me alone."

The lady's voice had raised to a screech, and all were watching, except for what Josh assumed were the hearing-impaired diners.

Mr. Sofa spoke first and was not complimentary.

"Silly old cow - she's always playing up, and what's more I think she wants to step out with me. She's always pestering me, she keeps trying to get me into her room. I might think about it if she had her own teeth. She also smells."

Josh shot a glance to David, who was trying not to laugh. Mr. Sofa saw and laughed heartily, the other two gave up and followed suit. They stopped when the attractive Thai nurse came over and said, "Now, now, boys. Seconds, Mr. Sofa?"

"Don't mind if I do Jade. Any chance of another bottle for my guests, or perhaps stronger?"

Mr. Sofa winked at his lunch guests which did not go unnoticed by Jade.

"Sorry Mr. Sofa, you know the rules. I would if I could."

"I bet you could, s'pose a bunk up is out of the question?"

David and Josh thought the same: that their new friend was trying to show off. The nurse pretended not to hear and got a colleague to collect their empty plates.

After seconds, Mr. Sofa also managed two bowls of vanilla ice-cream and a pot of lemon tea before he offered his two new friends a cigar each and led them outside into the residents' garden to smoke and relieve them of some cash via a few hands of blackjack.

They were eventually rescued by the Rabbi, who happened to go outside for a smoke and scolded them for gambling on the Sabbath.

Mr. Sofa returned to the warmth of the building, leaving the others to discuss business or whatever they were discussing, deciding things had been said that he did not want to know about. It was also time for his regular afternoon nap.

Josh, amassing losses to the old man and irritated by David taking the piss out of his poor blackjack run, left the heated religious chat David and the Rabbi were having and walked back to the car park and hopefully Stumpy.

The Volvo was there, as was Stumpy occupying the driver's seat, naturally smoking, and reading - or should that be gawping at a scantily clad woman in - *Men's Health* magazine. Stumpy jumped as Josh opened the front passenger door and got in.

Stumpy glared at him and responded with, "This one is one of ours and she's as good as she looks, and she knows what to do with that perfect mouth."

"Yeah, I can see the cold sore on her upper lip. How's your cock?"

"That's a mole Yiddo, you wouldn't say no."

"If you've been there I would. Take me back to the apartment, I need a rest – it could be a long night."

"Planning some fun with the Princess?" Stumpy gave a yellow-toothed nicotine grin and continued. "You're safe there - I would never touch her."

"Don't knock it 'til you tried it."

They both laughed as the engine struggled into life, although Josh did not like the undertone of racism.

Trouble with Mercedes...

Josh quietly contemplated his last night with Lydia before his return to London and Rachel, and the respect his peers would give him with his new position. He arrived safely back to an empty, clean apartment: no Lydia, but her scent lingered in the air. He turned the flat-screen TV on and switched to Sky Sports News to catch up with his first love, football and Spurs. It was the same as usual with conjecture on who Spurs would sign in the upcoming transfer window. He turned it off the moment Arsenal was mentioned. Pondering on his team, he realised his seat at White Hart Lane would be empty as he had a seat reserved on a train journey home.

Bored, he called Rachel, but cut her short when she chatted constantly about how wonderful her gay stylist was. Later, after pouring himself several whiskies and discovering an old western on an obscure Sky channel, he fell into a well-deserved sleep.

Josh woke with a start, his football dream disturbed by the sound of "Glory, Glory, Tottenham Hotspur" – his ringtone.

The room was dark as the sunlight had turned into night. Fumbling for the phone, he missed the call. He glared at the unlisted telephone number on the dark screen. The caller did not leave a message. His eyes focused on the time, it read 9:30 p.m.

He raised himself up from the settee still half asleep and decided it was time for a "shit, shave and shower" before his journey to Pepper Wilder.

Thirty-five minutes later, sitting comfortably back on the settee and sipping another whisky, his mobile again disturbed his peace and quiet. This time, however, the unlisted number left a message on his voicemail. Josh pressed the voicemail icon and heard a female voice, clearly in trouble. He did not recognise the voice but decided they needed help, whoever it was. The voice left a partial address before being cut off. He called David.

David was at the apartment within twenty minutes of receiving his call.

Five minutes after that, they were in David's Jaguar driving at speed to another modern apartment block in Bury. David listened to the voicemail on arrival at Josh's apartment. The voice belonged to Mercedes. She was in the apartment block and David knew she was likely in difficulty with an off-record punter.

All outside-venue punters were supposed to be vetted and verified by Lydia, who naturally took her own cut from such transactions. Having access to police records of "wrong'uns" was a bonus for everyone's safety. She had a contact that she had developed over the last few years after rescuing an officer from a comprising predicament. She also considered it fun, fucking an officer or two for continued information, occasionally in role-play: Lydia the prostitute arrested by two uniformed officers in a hotel bar, with being shagged senseless as the required sentence.

Some of the other club dancers ran their own personal girlfriend experience online service, all helped and set up by Lydia, without issue. It was clear that Mercedes had yet again tried to cut Lydia out of the equation. Mercedes, like the others, ran her own personal services on the internet. Lydia took a small percentage, actually slightly lower than the others at the request of the family due to Mercedes and the Vamp's high earnings at Pepper Wilder.

David used his own key fob to enter the building, Josh calling the lift as David was collared by the concierge who was telling tales of an unsavoury character who arrived earlier. The lift arrived and the pair hurriedly got in. They got out on the second floor of the six-floor block and turned left. Josh could see an apartment door ajar and knew this meant trouble. Both hurried their pace. David, without a word, entered first with Josh in tow, both creeping in gingerly, not knowing what to expect. The hallway was in semi-darkness: a compact space adorned with copy photos of David Bailey's popular work, which gave the hall a nightclub-like a feel. Josh stopped for a second catching a glimpse of a certain woman reverse-sitting open-legged on a dining chair with her modesty covered by the backrest. David gave out a minuscule hiss uttering.

"Come on, watch the floor lamp."

Josh responded like a scolded schoolboy.

On entering the living room, they discovered a disaster zone. The black TV screen was hanging off the wall, a table, smashed, with two broken champagne flutes in smithereens spread over the light-coloured carpet, mixed in with the contents of a broken bottle of Moët and white powder which Josh took to be cocaine seemingly everywhere. A female voice weeping and groaning coming from within the apartment was the only audible sound.

Both men followed the sound. Josh cracked open the mock-oak door spattered with blood on the inside. His eyes were drawn to the crumpled mess of Mercedes Nelson in the corner of the bedroom. She was curled up in the foetal position, moaning quietly, dressed only in her work undergarments - beside her, a blood-covered broken champagne flute. She looked up at Josh sobbing, giving a hint of recognition, eyes puffy, makeup smudged - not sultry as usual.

“Josh, I've made a mistake. I thought he was going to kill me. Lydia will. Please don't tell her.”

Mercedes’s uncontrollable sobbing was too much for David.

“You deal with her, I'm gonna check around,” he said.

David left the bedroom to check the apartment out and found the bathroom, treading on and breaking one of Mercedes high-heeled shoes, finding the blood pooled around the sink pedestal, the pink sink and matching bath full of bloody handprints. The other high heel was face down in the pool: not litres, but enough to indicate that the owner of the blood was in need of some medical attention. David did not touch anything except his own mobile to photograph the scene, making sure not to leave his own bloody footprints. Approaching the half-open window, looking out he saw bloody finger marks on the outside pipes and crumpled grass in the garden below. He pressed his mobile, and once the phone was answered simply said, "Clean up the team at Mercedes's home, please. Only the trusted Wilder mob. Tell them there will be a bonus."

Leaving the address to avoid confusion, he closed the call and returned to the bedroom, asking Josh, "Can you clean her up? What a mess. The Wailer team will sort the flat."

David's tone was abrupt in its nature and to Josh, it sounded like a demand.

Josh did not argue, remembering that David was one of his bosses.

"Yeah mate, no problem. She's alright, it's just superficial. I'll clean her up and call Lydia."

David acknowledged thanks and left, leaving his car keys. Josh heard him telephone Stumpy as he left the apartment.

Mercedes whimpered, "Please don't call Lydia. I promise I won't do it again."

Josh knew he had no choice but tried to reassure her that he would sort Lydia out. Mercedes grabbed his hand, squeezing it in an appreciative way. Josh cleaned her wounds after collecting TCP and cotton wool from the bathroom, ignoring the blood and disarray it held. Mercedes's long legs were covered in blood and cuts. Gently rolling down her stockings and removing her suspenders, Josh was a little surprised that she was shy and relatively coy, for a party girl. He felt the smoothness of her skin as he tended to her wounds. Mercedes whimpered as Josh dabbed at the cuts with TCP.

Smiling at Josh, Mercedes, in between sobs, said, "Thank you, Josh; you're so, so kind."

"Don't be silly, it's what friends do," he responded, as he discovered her birthmark and the reason for her shyness.

It was a large birthmark on the back and top of her lower left leg, which would usually be concealed in thigh length boots and dark stockings. Luckily for her, her Asian complexion hid most of the mark against her perfect skin. Mercedes, now more alert and thankful for her knight in shining armour, explained briefly what had occurred.

Josh, although himself a player, was disgusted by the events that had played out.

Her punter, a middle-aged white man, apparently a regular to Mercedes but not Pepper Wilder, who was previously just a dinner-and-fuck girlfriend experience, decided tonight was "experimental night" and wanted to explore her with a champagne bottle, particularly her anal cavity.

"I told him I'm not that kind of girl. I don't do anal in any shape or form and at first, I politely offered other sexual pleasures, but to no avail; he was not interested. He became steadily more aggressive after we did some Charlie. I knew he took too much, and it was then that he got really angry. He tried to force the bottle up me, Josh. I was scared. I ran to the bathroom after grabbing a champagne flute and stabbed him with the sharp broken end. It was his fault; he broke it as he tried to take it off me. Luckily, I got him first. I stabbed him in the neck with it. Fucking blood everywhere, it was spurting. I thought I'd killed him. He wasn't moving, Josh."

Mercedes was crying loudly, trying to compose herself. Josh put his arm around her as she managed to continue.

"It seemed like ages passed. He got up holding his neck, screaming "bitch", "slag", and worse. He kicked me hard, right in my fucking cunt, and stabbed my legs with my electric toothbrush. He then, thank God, jumped out the open window. I think I blacked out. I must have crawled into here, I can't remember. But Josh, tell Lydia it wasn't my fault."

Josh, embarrassed by hearing her story with her wounded nakedness, did the gallant thing by offering her a bathrobe suggesting a shower.

"Yeah, thanks, Josh. I'll feel better after. You're so nice," she said, kissing him lightly on his cheek.

Mercedes, alone in the bathroom, studied her injured body in the mirror, wincing at her appearance as she removed the remainder of her undergarments. Turning the shower on, she was sobbing at the realisation of her lucky escape. Tears flowed, as did her thoughts.

How did things get to this? It was supposed to never happen again.

Mercedes' mind focused on her past as the hot rain of the shower burned her wounds and pride. Up until five years ago, she was a happy-go-lucky graduate of Wolverhampton University, where she achieved a First-Class degree in psychology, finding local employment before her graduation ceremony. This was when things first started to go wrong - looking back, badly wrong. It was meeting the wrong lover. It was her first full-blown lesbian affair with a much older, domineering woman who also happened to be head of the department.

Stepping out the warm shower, still stinging, she looked at her cleansed long legs with their cuts and bruises, her inner thighs and groin sore from the earlier aggression.

"Pull yourself together, Mercedes Nelson. What would Lydia do? Would it ever fucking happen to her?" She said this out loud, while staring at her image in the mirror.

"Learn from Lydia - she's top girl for a reason. Get close to her, be her friend. Be her lover. Fuck her hard.

Don't screw her around. Yes, Lydia is a bitch; but that kiss…"

Mercedes felt an erotic mixture of pain and lust seeping from within, her nub taking over her earlier battle. Staying in front of the mirror, her hands gently served in self-exploration, fingers gliding in, finding her silkiness amongst her bruises as a sheen of juices enveloped her digits. Eyes half-closed in expectation, she desired more. Her breathing became heavy, fingers stimulating her clitoris as her womanly juices flowed towards her build-up, convulsing wildly as fingers encircled and rubbed against her own seduction. She watched herself in the mirror, slightly frowning and then pouting as she got through the pain, concentrating on her pending orgasm, its powerful delirious contractions forcing her body to quiver as it shot through her being, finally spasming in pure lustful ecstasy, mouthing, "Lydia, fuck me."

Mercedes watched her juices flow out her slit, tasting a mixture of herself and shower water as she came down from her climax. She grabbed a towel from the heated towel rail, enjoying its warmth as she wrapped it around her, beginning to feel better even with her deranged past creeping back into her head.

Remembering the older lover, being introduced to her oldest son, discovering a renewed interest in inappropriate men and the wrong drugs. First experimenting with marijuana, heroin, and finally crack-cocaine. The degree had taught her nothing. Mercedes submitted to the son, cutting herself off from her first lover. The son controlled her with drug fixes, utilising her dependence as a wedge against his mother. He abused her drug-addled body whenever he pleased, sharing her to whoever desired as long as they paid. Her saviour, an acquaintance of the mother, took pity on her instead of screwing her, paying for a month's treatment in a drying-out clinic, providing her with a flat on her release - rent-free for three months, no strings attached. Mercedes' saviour died a year later from prostate cancer.

Dabbing at her eyes, understanding the chances he had given her, she vowed to do better at protecting herself. Leaving the bathroom, she called out to Josh, thanking him, saying she felt much better and telling him to help himself to a drink while she dressed.

Lydia, Mercedes, and a Vamp...

Returning to her bedroom, sitting on the bed she thought about the night ahead and what to wear, and how to thank Josh for his help. She popped pills - painkillers to ease the pain and help endure the night and Lydia's likely abrupt orders. She was still worried if Josh would be able to pacify her nemesis.

Josh, meanwhile, oblivious to time, had slipped into what some would call a “power nap”, when Mercedes tapped him on the shoulder.

"I've called Pepper Wilder. They are sending a car. I'm supposed to be on my pole with the Vamp at 2:00 a.m.”

Mercedes had regained her composure from earlier, pushing the event to the back of her mind, especially as the pain between her thighs had subsided. She looked forward to seeing and dancing with the Vamp. Josh decided she was back to normality, or at least giving a good impression, looking stunning in a white low-cut short dress with black sheer stockings set off by thigh-length boots. Josh decided that she was good enough to devour, and it would be disingenuous to ignore as her perfect form glowed within the lights of the apartment. Josh remembered his promise, forming a plan on how to have Mercedes and pacify Lydia. He did not have any pangs of guilt in regard to Rachel while he concentrated on other available pussy.

"I haven't forgotten, love. I will tell Lydia that you simply had an intruder. I'm sure David will play ball, but I suggest no more punters, not behind Lydia's back anyway."

Mercedes realised this was going to cost and realising blatantly hitting on Lydia may help her cause in more ways than one, replied, "Sure, maybe we can party with her and go from there."

She hugged Josh, allowing him to briefly feel her delights as he certainly liked what he saw. She pulled back as his manhood reacted to the intimacy.

Mercedes immediately thought of her private session in the bathroom, brought on by his stiffness and that short deep kiss from Lydia, her brain and essence focusing on a potential threesome with Josh and Lydia. However, it perturbed her slightly as these days she only participated in threesomes with her partner, the Vamp, a continuing arrangement for the last four months.

"Let's wait downstairs in the lobby. I need some cigarettes, there's a Tesco Express attached to the building."

What she did not tell Josh was that she needed fresh batteries for her small bullet vibrator, an item she always carried. A tool of the trade you might say.

Josh agreed. He was running low himself and the e-cigarettes did not really do it for him. On the way out, Josh's eyes again focused on that photograph.

Both were silent in the lift, watching each other like a hungry lion eyes a wildebeest; but who was the prey? Josh watched as Mercedes produced a small mirror from her white clutch bag, withdrawing a small clear package from under her skimpy dress, placing a small amount of cocaine onto the mirror. She did not cut lines, licking her thumb placing it on the mirror.

“Want some?" she asked playfully, erotically sucking on her thumb.

The lift arrived at its ground floor destination.

Josh said nothing, staring at her curved mouth as it sucked on her thumb. Her playful temptation too great, he pulled her in, caressing her curves, removed her thumb, replacing it with his mouth, Mercedes mouth greedily inviting his.

They snapped apart as the lift doors opened, as if old acquaintances. He followed her to Tesco, enjoying her confident gait, hips swivelling from side to side. On entry, they separated into different shopping aisles. Well, Mercedes did, as Josh made for the cashier to purchase two packets of Marlborough. He paid with cash as the Mercedes S-Class arrived, pulling up directly in front of the store's main entrance. The professional driver in courtesy was standing as if to attention by the rear door as Josh left the store.

Josh did not enter the luxury car, instead lighting a cigarette from his fresh packet and confirming to the driver he was with Mercedes who would be there in a jiffy. He stubbed his cigarette out underfoot as Mercedes, with her head up, strutted towards him, her boobs seemingly leading the way.

The chauffeur stood at his post, avoiding eye contact with both as Josh said, “After you, madam.”

“Don’t mind if I do” she responded, as she set foot into the car in a gracious and well-mannered way. The chauffeur, taking his leave, walked steadily around the rear of the vehicle to his driver's seat, allowing Josh to make his companion comfortable before entering from the rear door behind the driver's seat. The chauffeur confirmed the destination as Pepper Wilder and the pair settled deep into the car’s sumptuous leather seats, with Josh stretching and yawning in comfort.

"Driver, can you do us a favour, mate, and stop when we are two minutes away? I fancy a smoke and a walk,” Josh asked courteously.

The driver acknowledged this, with Mercedes smiling in appreciation. She did not want an interrogation and the usual subsequent giggles from her work colleagues, especially not the beady eye of Lydia.

The car stopped as requested, with Josh alighting the vehicle with a “see you” to Mercedes. He watched it drive off down the street towards the club’s neon signs as he lit his cigarette and took his short stroll under the watchful eyes of the streetwalkers.

“Business love, do you want a date?” called one of them, shouting a deliberate sexual offer.

Josh ignored them. From a distance they looked half reasonable, but as he ambled passed them, he could see that many were skin and bone with a dead, vacant look you gain from long-term drug use. They were still offering themselves, almost in unison, as he watched Mercedes leave the car.

Josh approached Pepper Wilder’s door as another vehicle arrived, dropped, and drove off, the doorman still holding the door open. Josh acknowledged him politely and walked straight into Simon as he chatted to a red-headed scantily clad dancer by the cloakroom. Simon turned his attention to Josh.

"Evening. Good to see you. Gather it's your last one before you head back to the big bad smoke.”

“Yeah mate, likewise. She's a bit tasty,” Josh said this as the redhead shimmied off, allowing Josh a view of the bright tiger tattoo on her thong covered arsecheek.

The redhead heard the remark, turned, growled and winked suggestively.

“You can squeeze me arse anytime, darling,” she responded.

“I'll find you a table and some company. I'm sure Lydia will do, unless you're bored with her already,” continued Simon. Josh smiled at the mention of her name and Simon continued: “I've squared it with Lydia. She thinks Mercedes scared off an intruder. David told me all about it: and by the way, thank you for sorting it out."

"No prob, it was my pleasure."

Simon escorted Josh upstairs to a VIP Booth, and once seated, Simon left to attend to other matters, but not before summoning a waitress. Josh took his seat, choosing the garish red upholstered three-seater sofa and taking in his immediate surroundings. He accepted a single malt from the arriving cocktail waitress and requested Moët with two glasses. The waitress ambled off as Josh relaxed with his glass and enjoyed watching the dancers on their poles with their bodies gyrating in time to the music. He noted it was nearly 2:00 a.m. on his new Rolex, and like the previous night the atmosphere was heated with a mixture of testosterone and female hormone arousal. He watched as Mercedes took a bow before launching into her seductive routine around her pole alone, dressed in nothing more than a thong and thigh-length boots. He did wonder where her partner in crime was. He didn't notice the hand that slapped him until it made contact with the back of his head, the cocktail waitress sniggered as she appeared with a tray, glasses and champagne sitting in its ice bucket, placing the glasses on the table. The same hand that clouted him lifted the bottle popped the cork, its owner exclaiming that it had come.

"Shall I pour, sir?" Josh was slow to answer as he was busy rubbing his head.

“Evening Lydia,” he said, lifting his filled champagne glass. “I bet you wish you were coming like the bottle.”

Breathing in her distinctive Chanel and coconut body lotion, he took in her curvature, tightly wrapped inside a leather catsuit, her nipples obviously erect as they fought to escape their confinement.

Lydia sort of huffed and sat down opposite him on a red comfy armchair, partially and deliberately blocking his view of the dancers.

Josh took the hint, ogling her curves and teasingly said, "Bet you would look good down there riding a stiff pole,” pointing to the dancers who were now provocatively winding their slender forms around their poles, the one closest to Mercedes performing some form of acrobatics as Mercedes rubbed her privates up and down the pole, eyeballing them. She winced slightly from the earlier beating but hid her pain from all. More painkillers were required.

Lydia huffed, pointing at the acrobat, and beckoned her up. The dancer obliged and was beside her after negotiating the stairwell.

"Hey, I'm Angel,” she said, looking directly at Josh. She placed an elegantly gloved hand on his, and he, the gentleman, took it, kissing the back of her hand.

Lydia spoke before Josh uttered a word.

"Angel, darling, can you dance alone tonight?”

Angel knew disobeying Lydia was not on the menu, and meekly acknowledged her order by kissing Josh on the cheek.

"See you soon sweetie - a real gentleman."

Josh intentionally ogled Angel's behind as she walked away from the booth, flashing her a warm smile in the full knowledge it would inspire Lydia's lecherous response to himself and Mercedes. Lydia, on the other hand, gave her a cat-like stare with Angel reacting like a scared kitten backing away from its mother. Angel felt the loss of her partner and decided on an extended break from her pole. She felt Josh's eyes on her, but more importantly felt Lydia's eyes piercing into her as she left.

Lydia sipped from her glass and saw that Josh watched Angel's behind as it disappeared down the stairwell. Lydia, needing his attention back suggestively asked,

"How would I look on there? Shall I dance with Mercedes, what do you think? Do you want to play with us, or do you want to watch us perform?"

Lydia was in full teasing mode, and it would not hurt to mess with Mercedes's head as she was not sure about the break-in story. More likely she was earning on the side and had come unstuck. Lydia also had an urge to kiss and taste her. The teasing kiss in front of the boys the other night had turned her on. Mercedes mouth tasted sweeter, somehow different from the other girls. Lydia desired more. Besides, it was Josh's last night, and she intended to give him a going away gift. Josh without a doubt had his eye on Mercedes, and besides, she knew of the Vamp and Mercedes's promise.

The pair sat silently, not really looking at each other, but watched the other's body language as they ogled the nearly naked dancers. Josh, continually seeking attention, slurped his champagne and helped himself to another without offering Lydia a top-up. Lydia, allowing him to persist with his annoying behaviour, decided to act on her previous taunting words. Picking up the half-empty bottle, she left the booth and sexily walked down to the lower level, directly to a cavorting Mercedes. Josh watching intently as predicted. She handed the bottle to Mercedes, who willingly drank from the bottle and caressed it as she danced. She was giving the bottle head, allowing the champagne to flow down her chin as patrons gathered excitedly around her podium. She was encouraging her audience, directly pouring the cold champagne onto her breasts, her nipples standing to attention against the cold as she lathered the expensive alcohol focusing on her areola. Hands holding twenty and fifty pound notes were shoved into her thong and scattered onto the podium, with one hand managing to find her shaved region before being forcibly removed by Lydia, but she allowed the willing hand to undo the front zip on her tight-fitting catsuit, stepping out of it slowly in seduction. The hand was returned to its owner after unzipping, allowing a feel of Lydia's escaped free breasts, but not before Lydia playfully sucked Mercedes' forefinger whilst looking directly at Josh upstairs, who was watching eagle-eyed. Lydia, naked except for her white thong, took the bottle from Mercedes and teased the watching crowd by sliding it up and down Mercedes's inner thighs as Mercedes stood back, erect against her pole with her long firm legs wide to the cheers and money throwing punters. Pouring the remaining contents inside her thong, she began playfully rubbing it in. Mercedes, enjoying the experience, took control of the bottle and rubbed it gently over her own increasing wetness. She was beginning to lose control as her fingers slipped inside her just-about-hidden pussy, grinding increasingly against them, realising after a look from Lydia that she was getting into illegal territory. With a pre-orgasm moan, she passed the bottle back to Lydia who caressed and teased it with her mouth, enjoying the subtle taste of Mercedes, whilst slowly moving to the vibe of the music. She finished her act and handed the empty bottle to the closest punter who returned the favour with a handful of notes. Lydia whispered to Mercedes.

"Freshen up and join us upstairs in the red booth to give Josh a night he won't forget."

Mercedes, in her aroused state, agreed and French kissed her to the final thrill of the punters and the hidden annoyance of her girlfriend, who had seen the whole act from a safe distance whilst performing a lap dance on a moody punter who could not manage a hard-on. The Vamp was seething, as to her this looked like more than just a clubbing act.

Josh requested a fresh bottle of champagne from a passing cocktail waitress as he ascertained both would soon be joining him.

Lydia changed back upstairs in her office as Mercedes entered the regular changing room, where she noticed Angel crying in a discreet corner. Mercedes, as any decent human being would, enquired as to the reason. Angela, sobbing, acknowledged her workmate and began to cry, with tears flowing down her pretty face. Mercedes walked over to her discreet corner.

“Tell me, Angel, what’s wrong? Tears aren’t for Angels.” The room’s air conditioning forced a shiver as she spoke in her barely clothed body. Angel, with a Pepper Wilder towel draped around her slender body, explained her woes.

“I was feeling down as two separate punters couldn't get an erection during my lap dance and one grassed me to Lydia.”

“Were they pissed?” asked Mercedes.

Sniffing between tears, Angel resumed her tale.

“Err no, no worse than usual. I gave head to one after a tit wank and his little dick still hardly moved.”

Mercedes acknowledged the Vamp as she appeared

in the changing room, holding a bunch of notes.

The Vamp kissed her lover on the lips and said, “hi” to Angel. Seeing her tears and catching the drift of the conversation, she left them alone.

Angel continued: “The one that complained to Lydia lied. He said I didn’t touch myself in the way he wanted; he said that I said, ‘I don't do head’. You know me, honey, we've done plenty of blowjobs together loads of times. I can’t give head on a prick that's no larger than an inch, it’s not my fault.”

“What’s really going on Angel? We have all experienced such men.”

Angel, after some persuasion, got the real story out.

“The Turk, my boyfriend, he's dead. He burnt to death in a car, but it wasn’t his. Something ain't right. I think he was murdered. I know they are saying that, but I’m sure it wasn’t the slapper they arrested.”

Mercedes had heard about the incident, but not knowing the Turk, had not given it any thought.

“Are you sure? Why do you think that?”

“One of the outside club pros said he was a drug dealer. He wasn't.”

“Don’t believe all you hear, you know what them girls are like,” Mercedes interjected, trying to calm her down.

The Vamp, listening from her makeup station, came over and offered Angel her hip flask.

“Uncle Jack will help. Here, have some.”

Angel accepted the offer and took a long swig, holding the flask to her mouth with shaking hands. Mercedes assisted and lightly held Angel's left wrist as she drank.

After Angel's third gulp, Mercedes took control of the flask, drinking some herself before handing it back to the Vamp.

“Go on Mercedes, I’ll look after her. Don't you have a booking with Lydia and that Josh? Go get changed.”

The Vamp was being sly. She suspected what Mercedes was up to and was jealous, to say the least.

“Yeah, you’re right lover, I'm already in trouble. You heard about my break-in; I don't think that bitch believed me. If it wasn't for that new guy, what's his name?”

“Josh, I think. David was there too,” answered the Vamp.

“Yes. Anyway, I’d better dress. Don't want to keep ’em waiting. Can you look after Angel?”

Angel was sobbing again, muttering “It wasn't that poor girl - I'm sure it was someone else.”

The Vamp kissed Mercedes before turning her attention to Angel. Mercedes left them to it and on passing the Vamp’s make up station, snorted the remaining line of cocaine the Vamp had cut and left for later.

“Thanks, hun, it helps my bruises. Speak later.”

The Vamp, looking up from her chair next to Angel,

responded, “Anytime, hun.”

The drug immediately hit Mercedes brain and pussy as she sat down to freshen her eye make-up.

Hidden From View...

Josh took a sip from his third glass of champagne as Lydia pulled back the red booth's curtains, revealing herself. Josh saw her but averted his eyes towards the dancers below to get a rise out of her. Lydia stood there quietly as if thinking, sucking on her e-cigarette. Dressed for her new game, out of the catsuit, she was clad in a tight white button-down blouse, black tight mini-skirt and matching stockings. She was looking sophisticated, secretarial, in a pair of glasses.

"You need me to take down a letter, Mr. Goldstein?"

Josh understood her game.

"Yes, Miss. You look very nice today. Please take a seat and help yourself to a glass of champers - and pour me one."

"Yes sir, right away."

Lydia carried out the request and sat down, crossing her legs beside Josh on the armrest of the sofa, taking a sip from her glass.

Josh looked her up and down.

"I'm waiting for you, miss."

Lydia slowly placed the glass onto the red glass table, asking, "Have you a pencil, sir? Mine's in the secretarial pool."

"You're supposed to be prepared. What kind of secretary are you? You deserve to be punished."

"Yes, sir." Lydia stood up and bent over, her tight skirt-clad arse close to Josh's face. "Don't hurt me, sir. Be gentle."

Her skirt had ridden up to reveal the flesh of her behind. Josh did as expected and slapped her pert behind six times, each slap harder than the last.

"More, sir, I need to be punished harder."

Josh agreed and said, "This is not the first time, is it, Lydia? You're always late, you're never prepared. What do you suggest I do? I should sack you."

"No please don't, sir! I need this job. What do you need me to do? I'll do anything you ask. Shall I dance for you?"

"Good idea, Lydia, that's a start. Put that toy cigarette down first."

Lydia did as asked, producing Josh's Zippo lighter from underneath her shirt.

"I found this, sir," she said, handing Josh his lighter.

"Thank you, Miss. You were saying..."

"What sort of dance? Do you want a sexy dance? Shall I strip dance?"

"What do you think Lydia? You keep letting me down, it really depends on how much you need the job."

"I'll do my sexy erotic club thing, my pulling dance. It always works."

With that Josh gave her a thumbs up. Lydia began to dance slowly at first, hands undoing her blouse buttons, revealing a lace plunge bra that did a perfect job of lifting her cleavage. Pulling her unbuttoned blouse over her head, she revealed her firm flat torso, tantalising Josh as she swayed. Her hands began pushing up her cleavage before cupping and embracing her breasts as if they belonged to a lover. Josh concentrated on Lydia's hands and elegant fingers as they teased her nipples.

"Go on, bitch," he said, "you know you want to pinch them. Fucking pinch, use your thumb and forefinger. Do as you're told."

Lydia responded by pinching them hard, relishing the thrill as the pain shot through her body. She felt the tension slowly build between her legs, having every intention of teasing Josh to his limits. She knew Mercedes was waiting outside the booth's curtains. Part of her plan to have both here and now, but not quite yet.

Enticing Josh by bending over closer to him, giving him an appealing view of her cleavage, she continued to caress and compress her assets, looking at him directly, teasing his focus as she skimmed her belly button before slipping a hand inside her skirt.

"How are my job prospects?" she said while pushing her hand within.

Josh answered, "Improving, but only slightly, keep impressing me."

Lydia removed her hand from within and tasted herself by sucking on her index finger.

"Want some?" she said, with her finger still in her mouth.

She placed her hand back inside her skirt, but this time lifting it, allowing a brief view of crotchless knickers, inserting an index finger into her depths.

"Much, much better," Josh said, encouraging her finger to explore.

"Want a taster?"

Josh nodded in anticipation.

Lydia did as requested, removing her finger allowing Josh a taste of her bud.

"Do I deserve a drink now?" she queried, intentionally looking frightened.

"You may, but do it yourself. Pour me one first."

"Okay, straight away, sir."

Lydia bent over after straightening her skirt, covering her womanhood, and lifted the Moët, deliberately allowing it to slip out of her hand onto the red-carpeted floor of the booth. In her dummy frightened state, she got down on all fours, arse protruding, knocking the table with just enough force to topple and break a champagne flute, its contents spilling onto the table, her arse still raised in an effort to collect the fallen bottle.

Josh reacted as she hoped.

"Fucking stupid secretary! Look what a two and eight you've made, fucking get a cleaner."

Josh at this point was not sure if this was a real

kerfuffle or a deliberate part of her game.

“Sorry, sir, I’ll get one”, replying breathlessly as she slowly and amorously stood back up, adjusting her glasses to sit further down her nose, whipping back the booth curtains.

“Will this maid do?”

Josh averted his gaze to the wonder behind the curtains, appreciating that Lydia's earlier act was part of her salacious entertainment.

The wonder was Mercedes standing with her legs apart, dressed provocatively in a white latex figure-hugging mistress maid outfit, her long legs in matching fishnets. Lydia turned to face him, Josh's bulge between his legs evident to all. Mercedes entered and closed the booth curtains.

“You rang, madam. I’m at your service.”

Lydia turned to face Mercedes, feeling her own throb of desire.

“Yes, the table needs cleaning. Get scrubbing, you little scrubber. Bend over and clean it properly.”

In truth, Lydia was a little taken aback. The maid's outfit and the scent of Mercedes certainly did it for her, feeling an instant urge to grab her and spread her body over the table. Lydia held her urge in check as Mercedes bent over the table in an effort to clean, allowing Josh and Lydia a full view of her slender legs and undergarments.

“What do you fink you’re doing?” demanded Josh,

playing the game. “Did I tell you to clean the table?”

“Err no, sir. What is your command?”

“Punish bad Lydia, she needs a spank.”

“Yes, sir.”

“Lydia, bend over now; that's an order, you dirty slut!”

Lydia did as asked, lifting up her skirt, revealing her arse, slightly red from the earlier slapping.

Mercedes was eager to please; the prospect of taking control of Lydia even for a minute was a thrill. She slapped Lydia’s behind hard, with the back of her hand.

Lydia squealed in pain, realising Mercedes was taking the piss a little bit. The pain, however, increased her desire. She needed more.

“Slap me harder, Josh said I’m naughty and a dirty slut.”

Mercedes looked up at Josh, as if requiring guidance.

Josh, enjoying the moment, gave a thoughtful look, flicking his Zippo, his desire blatant.

“Yes, Mercedes, two more slaps, but first come here. Lydia, don't move,” he demanded.

Lydia did as asked, staying bent over, relishing the lingering sensation of her tingling arse and throbbing groin. She knew what was coming, as it was her idea. Mercedes took two steps to where Josh sat. She could not resist Josh’s swelling between his legs, tracing his thickness up and down his shaft. Josh was radiating heat from her warm touch. She looked directly into Josh's eyes begging for pleasure and enjoying the feeling of control over both, kissing Josh's mouth, knowing Lydia could hear the sounds of their intimate kiss. Mercedes began guiding his hand up her short maid's skirt, to her crotchless knickers and her succulent eager femininity, gasping as fingers lingered before ravaging her waiting slit. Lydia, still bent over, stood up, toying with her own budding wetness as Josh fingered Mercedes, gazing directly at her. Lydia could see Josh's excitement as she grinded against her fingers. Mercedes moved with her, mimicking her movement.

Lydia was controlling their every moment, which was her intention. She was going to have Mercedes first. Josh could wait; she required him full of his seed and making him watch would increase his load. After all, he was going to share with them both.

Lydia, further enforcing control, said to the fingering pair, "Aren't I still a dirty whore who needs punishment?"

"Agreed, this is part of your discipline. Stop fingering yourself and watch, I want your hands behind your back. Do it now," Josh said brusquely.

Lydia meekly obliged, putting her hands behind her back.

Mercedes undid Josh's shirt buttons to expose his firm chest, slowly licking her way down his torso until kneeling, totally aware that Lydia could see her arse cheeks, and Josh a bird's eye view of her exposed glossy crotch.

Josh started to force her head down onto his concealed cock. Lydia did as directed, controlling her urge and enjoying the image as her wetness increased. Mercedes wanted a large cock in her mouth, but withheld from undoing his fly, pretending to give head, loving that Lydia could only watch and not touch. Josh held Mercedes's head as she bobbed up and down, before bringing her face up and kissing her amorously, a finger exploring her increased wetness within her maid's skirt. He withdrew his mouth and eyed Lydia. Lydia, as an encouragement, undid her clasped hands from behind and erotically inserted three fingers inside her hidden crease.

"Naughty, filthy slut. You're in fucking trouble; I told you, no fingering. Bend over. Mercedes: three hard slaps please."

Mercedes removed herself and obediently obliged.

A much-needed cocktail waitress appeared with a fresh bottle of Moët, ignoring their game and handing each a full glass of bubbly. Fresh air from the briefly opened curtains wafted in, mixing with the heavy scent of sex. Lydia, recognising the rules of full-on sex in a public club space, suggested her office. She asked the waitress to carry the fresh bottle and glasses into her office. The cocktail waitress did as asked, secretly jealous that Lydia was about to indulge in another of her threesomes. Last time it was with two hunky, well-endowed men, and it was her privilege to help out - a woman in the right place at the right time. But as she was purely heterosexual, her involvement would not be required today.

The three followed Lydia into her office which she unlocked via a wall keypad. The waitress placed the silver Pepper Wilder tray onto a nearby side table, in full knowledge of the likely use of the main office table.

"Anything else, Miss Chipping?"

Josh stifled a laugh as he had not heard Lydia's surname before.

"No, thank you. That's all."

The cocktail waitress acknowledged and left discreetly, closing the office door behind her.

Lydia sat on the large sofa; Mercedes sat at the far end. Josh sat between them, briefly observing his surroundings. On the wall behind an image of a Wildebeest and naked lady sitting astride the animal's back. He also saw the many modern CCTV screens which covered the entire club, with two separate images on each.

One - the largest - was blank.

The smell of sex followed them into the office. Lydia, draining her glass, hungrily kissed Josh after placing his glass on the table. Her hand reached across him, brushing his hardness, and found Mercedes's inner fishnet clad thigh, touching her warmth between her eager open legs. Mercedes guided the pleasure into her crotch. She too smooched Josh, three tongues intermingled, sharing each other's exploration. Josh had one hand finding Lydia's fingers, joining them inside Mercedes, who was groaning while grinding against the added pleasure two different hands offer. Josh's other hand was finding Lydia's equally wet and engaged gyrating pussy. Mercedes then unzipped his fly, taking out his large bulging cock, feeling the tension within its skin as its red veins protruded in readiness.

Mercedes started to lick Josh's tip and opening.

Lydia was having none of it. She was first and as a distraction, picked up the TV remote, pressing play and immediately turning the blank screen on, showing one-on-one female action. The sex on the screen engaged Mercedes, watching the writhing bodies captured enthusiastically on the large screen. Lydia, also watching the images, took control of the other two, seating herself on her uncluttered office desk, her legs wide, her entrance brazen in its moisture. Josh's cock was jutting towards Lydia, Mercedes's inner lips engulfing Josh's digits. Lydia was fingering herself, watching the action on the screen. Josh whispered into Mercedes's ear, licking at her often-forgotten erogenous zone, sending instant electric pulses elsewhere.

Mercedes did not need asking twice. Raising herself, repositioned between Lydia's thighs, she began to gently taste and swirl her tongue against Lydia's excited juicy clitoris. Josh's view was obscured by Mercedes behind, so he did the only thing he could. He stood up and probed Mercedes from behind, using the bullet vibrator Mercedes produced earlier from her petite handbag. Lydia's face was contorting in pleasure. Both women gasped and moaned as one.

Lydia was needing to cum and wanted Josh's seed inside her mouth.

"I want your cock, ram it in my mouth now. I want it to cum when I do. Mercedes, eat me out, widen my cunt, fuck me with your tongue. Lick my clit hard. I've got to cum with Josh in my mouth. Josh, I want it now," Lydia shouted the words at both to succumb to her needs, almost incoherent but not to experienced love makers.

Mercedes, like Josh, did as ordered by opening Lydia's inner lips with her long fingers, allowing her slithering tongue to explore deeper and further. Mercedes, having her own urgent desire to cum, fingered herself as Josh positioned himself, available to Lydia's lusting demands.

Lydia spread herself onto the table, waiting for his cock as Mercedes brought her to near climax, licking her boss out. Lydia reached out to Josh's cock, with her tongue lapping at his tip as it stood thick and stiff over her face.

"I fucking told you, closer, ram it hard. I want it hitting my throat."

Josh could not resist his tease any longer and slammed his thick girth into her warm demanding mouth.

Mercedes's was breathing deeply, blistering in vocally charged sexuality, fully aware Josh's cock was inside Lydia's gasping mouth. Her tongue circled Lydia's clit, biting gently at first as Lydia's grinding turned into hurried urgency. Lydia was desperate with the luscious haste in her mouth and pussy, feeling Josh's cock build towards its arrival as she too got close.

It happened too soon; Josh shot deep into her throat just before Lydia exploded into Mercedes mouth, Mercedes arriving against her own fingers a second later. Warm spunk flooded into Lydia's mouth as Josh's dick pumped its load. Mercedes wanted her turn at his cream. She stopped licking and attacked the rapidly discharging cock filling Lydia's mouth. Its juice was seeping out her mouth as it throbbed and surged. Mercedes licked at his scrotum and partially available shaft. Her tongue began producing more cum as Josh pumped harder, having two mouths milking him. Lydia reached out her hands, finding Mercedes's breasts as they both built towards another orgasm. Lydia demanded his cum inside her mound, as well as her mouth.

Positions changed: Mercedes sat astride Lydia's face in reverse cowgirl as Josh slid her down the table to fuck her.

Unlike before, they all came together, Josh filling Lydia's pussy with his seed as Mercedes sucked and swallowed at Lydia's orgasm.

Lydia, being greedy and wanting more, allowed them to rest for thirty minutes. Then there were two separate hands on Josh's wilting cock as he fingered each of them whilst all three were back on the sofa watching the erotic film unfold, Josh again sitting between them.

There was no rest for him. He was soon stiff as the two women kissed and shared his shaft, their tongues colliding in unity, licking his length, fondling each other's nipples as they greedily shared his cock and scrotum. Josh began erupting into two open hungry mouths, Mercedes and Lydia shared and exchanged his cum in a deep, enflamed French kiss. All three continued to kiss until exhaustion took over their bodies, hot and sticky in after-sex.

Mercedes reacted first, thinking initially she was dreaming.

"Lydia, Lydia - your phone."

Lydia answered it on the sixth ring, her orifices and body sticky from the orgy, with a curt "Yes?"

As she listened to the call her sexual gratification face changed to serious business, its colour drained.

"I have to go - there's an incident in the dancer's room."

She did not say any more as Mercedes and Josh stirred, untangling their bodies from each other. Lydia hurriedly dressed into her secretarial clothes, minus her underwear and spectacles, and left the office. Josh looked at Mercedes, who appeared not to be bothered as she laughed, suggesting one of the girls had probably broken a nail and was in a strop. Josh accepted her explanation as she sat up on the floor, looking – unbelievably - still erotically charged in her ready-for-action crotchless knickers.

The porno was still playing on the screen, showing a mixed-sex orgy, which did not go unnoticed by either.

"Josh, we haven't done that yet. Wanna tit-wank?"

Well, what else could he say, especially as Mercedes positioned herself on the sofa, pouring the flat, but still cold champagne over her breasts, instantly stiffening her perfect nipples? Josh obliged her and positioned his stiff member between her wet breasts, supporting himself with hands on the back of the sofa. Mercedes lubricated him with the remains from the bottle, squeezed and fondled, working his cock between her tits.

"Fuck my tits, cream-pie me," she said, panting erotically, as she firmly slid his cock up and down her glands, her tongue reaching his tip. Josh slightly changed position, allowing her mouth to engulf more as she pushed her tits ever harder against him.

Josh gasped, withdrawing his cock from her mouth

as he partly shot over her face and gleaming wet breasts. Mercedes licked the cum from around her mouth while she massaged his hot spunk into her tits.

Panting she demanded, "Fuck my pussy, it's not had hard, thick cock yet!"

Angel of Death...

Lydia found the Vamp in tears outside the changing room.

"She's in there. She's dead. I thought I would check on her between dances, but I was longer than I thought. It's my fault."

Lydia comforted her by putting her arms around her slender waist and replied, "What do you mean it's your fault, darling?"

"I should have gone in and checked on her, she overdosed. I think she did herself in."

"No not Angel, she's not like that."

The Vamp continued looking whiter than usual.

"The feds are in there, we can't go in. Earlier she said her boyfriend was murdered."

Lydia, aware of the truth, was saying little as more plainclothes officers arrived including a pathologist and a forensic video specialist.

The first officer, in a courteous manner, introduced himself.

"Detective Constable Gallie with an 'I-E', not 'E-Y'. This room is now a potential crime scene until forensics are complete. Constable Davies is upstairs taking statements from all staff members and guests who may have spoken to the young woman.

"Let me see now." He referred to his notebook.

"Miss James: I understand her professional name is the Vamp. Is that correct, and who might you be?"

"Yes, that's right, officer. I manage the girls, and I'm Miss Lydia Chipping," she said, all thoughts of sexual gratification drained from her mind, replaced with genuine concern.

"I assume a gentleman's club has full CCTV coverage and membership lists of all guests present. Is that correct Miss?"

"Yes, Officer. Members check in on arrival. Gold members are allowed one guest, platinum up to three, except there is no coverage in here; the girls need their privacy. The screens are in my office, and the security room is along up there."

Lydia was pointing out the security door."

"Thank you, Miss Chipping, your doormen are very helpful and have closed the venue down. Patrons and staff can leave once interviewed. Regrettably it may take a few hours."

"I understand, Constable."

"It's Detective Constable, Miss. One of my officers will remain outside this door for security. Please can you wait upstairs to give your full statement? And can you take Miss James with you? May I suggest a drink to calm her down? She appears distraught. Lydia nodded and supported the Vamp as they did as instructed.

Lydia texted Mercedes's with a brief outline of the

circumstances, not mentioning Angel's death, as she did not want them to be found in flagrante, knowing it was likely they were enjoying each other's bodies.

Mercedes and Josh finished fucking, noticing the odd activity on the CCTV monitors after Mercedes had received Lydia's text. Dancers were not performing on their poles, patrons were looking ghost-like, uniformed police officers were milling around, chatting to both dancers and patrons. They dressed and as instructed walked down the stairwell, Mercedes unfortunately in her Maid's outfit.

The hub of Pepper Wilder was in confusion. Members were needing to leave for home. Some, with mistresses, would need excuses for spouses if names were mentioned in the press. A cabinet minister, found in a VIP Booth with several dancers and mistresses, was suffering a meltdown in the corner. He was drunk and rambling, saying he did not want to be the next Profumo and asking if he could leave. Simon was doing his best to calm him down. He pulled rank and persuaded a constable to take his statement early. The constable, on recognising the minister, obliged, realising the possible implications. Luckily, the minister was not in the company of Angel that night, but as a regular, knew of her.

Mercedes in her maid's outfit caused a stir amongst the young constables in the bright club lights, shimmering in her curvaceous form, especially her crotchless knickers, as she alighted the stairwell. Her statement was taken down out of sync by an over-excited policeman. She later confessed to the Vamp that knowing many uniformed eyes were on her was an unexpected turn on. The lucky constable took his time with her, going over her conversation with Angel earlier several times to make sure he got the facts written down right. Her overtly sexual nature was a clear distraction to the young naive officer. The Vamp and Mercedes did not mention the Turk, saying she was simply depressed after splitting up with her ongoing boyfriend. Josh, as directed by Gary, helped organise the order of statements taken from the members. Lydia organised the dancers.

The police allowed the patrons and staff to leave after individual statements were given, except for Simon, Gary, and Lydia, who were required to stay on the premises while the police forensic team finished their investigation in the dancers' changing room, and only after the sad removal of Angel's corpse, conveyed in a private ambulance to the police mortuary for examination.

On leaving, Josh noted the lack of street prostitutes, who he was sure must have fled as the police arrived. He walked around the corner to hail a black taxi for his journey back to his club apartment.

Rachel Prepares...

Back in London, Rachel, Josh's wife, woke early - too early - as Josh climbed into bed exhausted from the evening's rampant sexual activity and police attendance at the club.

She felt on top of the world, her "Ba'al" (literally meaning "the master") was expected later on today. Although not religious like her Sabba (grandfather), she always kept to her marriage vows, believing in the sanctity of marriage. Rachel suspected Josh of having several affairs during their marriage but turned a blind eye as long as he kept it away from the marital front door. Her brothers were just as bad and perhaps even worse. Josh did not ever beat her, he always did his best in providing, and yes, he was still in love with her. She could live with his indiscretions, especially as he had sexual needs that she could not bring herself to provide or perform.

After a long, invigorating morning read, Rachel, dressed in her daily housework clothing of comfortable oversized tracksuit bottoms and a black t-shirt, attended to her chores, including cleaning the kosher chicken for Josh's return. Kosher food was, to her, nicer than the usual - that is why she stuck to it, rather than for religious reasons. She felt lucky. The meat was always good quality as it was supplied directly by the family kosher warehouse, and usually delivered weekly. On the occasions she visited (the last time about two months ago) there was a "to-do" with a palate of broken kosher wine bottles being cleaned up on her arrival.

Sleep-deprived...

Josh, in Manchester, tossed and turned. He could not sleep despite being exhausted after finally getting into bed at 4:30 a.m. He had too much on his mind. His new job was exciting, but he was aware of the danger of getting nicked. The family did not specify how or why his new position became available after all this time he'd allowed in.

Temptation Beckons...

Rachel, cleaning the bathroom, was happy with her husband's new family role. She had instigated it, but it had taken several years of persuasion. Her only negative feeling was his regular "away days" to Manchester at the family's bequest. She knew only too well the club temptations, especially Lydia - or Delilah, as she preferred to call her. On the odd occasion they had met, she found that Delilah had a magnetism that drew all around her in, including herself. Rachel could not understand why, as she had never experienced such odd feelings towards another woman, even at university when drunk or slightly stoned. In fact, she had never strayed. Josh was her second partner. It was love at first sight and until meeting Lydia it had always been that way.

She cursed it out of her mind as she plugged the vacuum cleaner into an electric plug socket. Temptation was not her thing.

Sleep-deprived II...

Josh gave up trying to sleep around 8:30 a.m. The sunlight mixing with his hangover did not help. He decided to get up, shower, dress, and pack his case. He had plenty of time as he assumed Stumpy would drive him back to Manchester Piccadilly.

He thought about last night's threesome as he soaped his body down, paying extra attention to his sore red cock. Thankfully, Rachel would not notice it, nor the scratch marks on his torso, as they only fucked in in the dark. On his front were the claw-marks of Mercedes; his back was Lydia's handiwork when they fucked against the window in the living room.

Showered and dressed, he sat in the kitchen, drinking strong, fresh espresso after popping two strong headache pills and focusing his mind on Rachel.

Temptation Wins...

Neither Rachel's cursing nor vacuuming could get her weird thoughts out of mind. In fact, they got worse. She imagined her husband having sex with others in the family's London warehouse, fictitiously catching him in the act. Rachel could see him on his office desk enjoying fellatio. Her mind was not visualising with whom, just his expression of desire. She began recoiling in horror when the visualisation became her face. Her horror tortured her and then, unexpectedly, her pussy reacted as did her heart, pounding in her chest, her breathing increasing. Rachel's libido started sending electric desire through her body in anticipation. She detached the vacuum equipment in an effort to block her desire and hoover the stairs. Her yearning was increasing while attaching the crevice tool to the hose pipe. The equipment was vibrating in shaking, nervous hands. Sitting on the bottom stair, holding the attached pipe, her psyche was yearning for more. Envisioning his stiffness, the tool became Josh's phallus. Her head was focusing on the needs of her body, her vagina hot and sticky in its demand. All sense of her being changed in that moment. Losing control to her vagina, it urged her - it demanded action. Hands began hypnotically positioning the vibrating equipment between her legs over her tracksuit bottoms, her pussy demanding and throbbing to masturbation, heart pumping in an effort to get lungs filled with air, eyes closing in ecstasy. She was gasping as her intellect experienced longing and Josh's organ, her head filling with sexual filth, succumbing to desire, desperate for his penis in her mouth. Finally, she exploded onto her fingers, her hand inexplicably within her jogging bottoms. Rachel steadied her breathing as she came down from her hypnotic erogenous state. Switching the vacuum off, almost in shock discovering the wet knickers from pent-up lust, Rachel could not comprehend the reason why she had had such a lustful urge. Her ears reacted to lyrics from Simon And Garfunkel's "Bridge Over Troubled Water". Remembering who she was, she was back to boring old Rachel. She knew deep down she needed to pursue this new Rachel.

Josh, his head beginning to clear as the pills and four espressos did their work, had called Rachel three times. On the third call, twenty minutes after the first, she responded sounding strange, almost breathless.

"Hey Rachel, have you taken up jogging?" was his opening once she finally answered.

Initially, she was silent except for the sound of her laboured breathing.

Josh wondered if the phone signal was bad. He checked his smartphone; it showed four bars on the screen. It was not his end. He repeated the question.

"Hi Josh, darling. I was hoovering and dusting the

bedroom. I didn't hear my phone until I finished."

Josh was bemused. Rachel still sounded strange. He could not put his finger on it. Her voice sounded husky and sexy.

"You got a man in there?" he asked jokingly.

Rachel, in a still slightly after-climax state stuttered, "Err, err... just me and the Hoover."

As the words left her lips, she felt embarrassment as that was not what she meant to say. She could not believe she had actually masturbated, the first time since their marriage vows. She was feeling relaxed, as her climax had released pent-up desire and tension.

"Can't wait to see you, I've missed you."

Strange, Josh thought, as usually during a trip phone call, questions were unabating.

"Me too," he answered back.

Her further responses became her usual, though Josh still felt an air of female sexuality in her tone.

She cut the call off first. Again, this was unusual, but Josh was not unhappy with it as his head again began to throb.

Rachel also began to throb again, but not in her head. She had cut her husband short as her need to attend took over. In her imagination this time she was dressed in provocative underwear. Perhaps, she thought, she had time to visit Marks & Spencer's and shock her husband on his return.

Goodbye, Josh...

Josh, after the call, drank the last of his espresso and thought about Rachel who seemed to be sexually aroused. He put it down to the start of her menopause and the fact that she was missing him. His phone rang: the screen said Lemski Ltd. Josh remembered he had altered Lydia's name just in case Rachel checked his contacts list. They chatted briefly about Angel's death and what they would do to each other on his next visit. Lydia suggested using WhatsApp as a discreet way of communicating if he wanted to keep in contact. Josh agreed it made sense. She confirmed his ride to the station with her last comment.

"Perhaps I can ride you on your return - I always enjoy a well-hung stallion."

She hung up before Josh could respond.

His phone rang ten minutes later. It was a recorded WhatsApp video with a naked Lydia riding a large dildo, declaring, "I'm thinking of you as I ride my big toy."

Josh chuckled as his cock sprang to attention, and he watched it as Lydia continued to enjoy herself with numerous sex toys, finishing the recording after she orgasmed vocally and physically. After coming, she wiped the screen with her pussy-moist hand, saying with laughter, "This video will self-destruct in ten seconds"

Naturally, it was impossible for that to happen, and Josh erased as suggested.

His head at long last clear of its hangover, he decided this should be marketed and patented as a hangover cure.

A Wife Explores...

Rachel, returning from her shopping trip, admired her image in her new provocative lingerie through the mirrored bedroom wardrobe doors. Her breasts were firm and seductive in a way she had not seen before. It pleased her, particularly as it turned her on. Squeezing her breasts over the silky material, her nipples were sensitive to her light touch. Rachel refrained from going further, needing to keep her energy for Josh's arrival home.

Ride Home...

Josh answered the apartment intercom. It was Stumpy, as expected.

Twenty-five minutes later, the elderly Volvo arrived at Manchester Piccadilly Station. Josh bid Stumpy goodbye and after purchasing a Classic Car magazine, confectionery and a cheese sandwich, took his allocated seat on the train bound for London Euston.

Virgin Sexting...

Rachel, after preparing supper for her husband's return, decided they would eat in their small dining room with a bottle of red wine (instead of the usual: eating in front of the TV) and she would actively seduce her husband, dressed in one of her new sexy outfits. She was feeling nervous, as if on a first date, perceiving that it had been many years since she actively sought to seduce anyone.

Rachel had sought advice from the internet on how to reinvigorate the marital bed, reading avidly different articles on seduction techniques and how to pleasure your long-term partner. Slow seduction was her chosen course, hopefully leading to unusual, debauched activity. Understanding her own body's needs was also important for her own satisfaction and gratification. She had never been one to tell her partner what she wanted or enjoyed. Until earlier today she had never envisaged herself having sex with another, but after reading erotic content, lustful thoughts entered her mind. Perhaps Rachel was missing out on something.

Part of her seduction was sexting. Until reading about it on her laptop, she did not know it even existed. Now she was about to try to do it. Holding the mobile phone nervously in one hand, she was soaking in the perfumed bubble bath having already drunk three vodka shots in quick succession. Rachel decided on her wording and tapped in her first raunchy message.

"Hi, Josh. Guess where I am."

Reading the words slowly and deleting, deciding it was not erotic, she recalled her earlier reading on her laptop; reflecting, soaking in her hot bubble bath, relaxing with the harmony vodka offers. It worked: Josh's cock became her focus, imagining it stiff inside her; Josh gazing lovingly into her eyes as he made love to her slowly and passionately.

The advice worked. What stuck in her mind were the words "Be as explicit as you feel comfortable". She had read the first of the *Fifty Shades* trilogy after a friend suggested it and mulled over the remembered text to find something appropriate to use. She was sure she had read, "Show me how you pleasure yourself." or was it "Pull my hair as I want to feel you at the back of my throat." Rachel could not quite remember but thought the young graduate's name was Annabelle. She then decided it was not, but her name definitely started with an A. The words now stuck in her head, so she had her first words.

"I want your cock; I want to feel it at the back of my throat."

The words jumped at her from the phone screen. She was thinking about the words, being purposeful and direct, and with a sharp intake of breath, bravely pressed "send".

Josh, engrossed in an article about a classic Mini Cooper in the quiet train carriage, was distracted from his reading as his phone lit up with a message. He continued to the end of the paragraph before reaching for his phone which was sitting on the pull-out table.

He tapped the screen.

"I want your cock; I want to feel it at the back of my throat."

He assumed it was Lydia, until he looked at the sender details.

Josh looked again in disbelief. It was Rachel.

Rachel kept her phone in her hand, expecting an answer. The screen said her message had been delivered and read. She could not believe that she had sent a dirty text message; she could also not believe her vagina felt wet. It was not just bath wet, but aroused wet. Her mind thought of Christian in the book.

He is squirting massage oil into his hands. He is watching her, not A.

Her phone screen was still blank.

She decided to type another text.

"I don't want you to make love to me - I want you to fuck me, hard."

This time, not dithering, she pressed send.

Josh felt his phone vibrate in his hand. It was another text message from Rachel. He read it twice, not associating the words with his wife. She never swore, especially the word fuck - but it most definitely was her.

"Where do you want me to fuck you, in your mouth or pussy?"

Rachel received his response a second later. She was beginning to feel confident and was enjoying herself. Reading his text, she massaged her breasts with scented soap, pinching and encouraging her nipples, already alert and erect.

"I want both," was her returned text.

Josh read her text, imagining her wet. Re-reading his message and thinking about her text, he decided she must be pissed. He received another. This time it was a selfie of her hands massaging her breasts, looking alluring and erotic, nipples hard and wet.

He sent another answering her question and asking her another.

"In your mouth first, or do you want two; one in each?"

Rachel read his text. She had never thought of that before - was she repulsed or stimulated? She was not sure. Deciding his question was too extreme, she thought of something else. She was at least willing to experiment.

"First in my mouth as I caress myself."

Josh decided he had been too graphic and toned it down for his response.

"Sounds like a plan. Can I watch you now?"

Rachel drank her fourth vodka shot which was sitting on the bath rim panel surface. She could not bring herself to send a live video, she was not ready for that. She settled on cupping one breast, which was still covered in soap and bubbles, took a photo, and pressed "send".

Josh enjoyed seeing his wife's image and sent a final message.

"I want to slowly lick you all over."

Rachel responded with a red heart icon, conceding afterwards to herself that she had taken pleasure in her first sexting session, and as her reading suggested, it did turn her on.

"I will wait for your safe return." Rachel was not sure why she spoke those words out loud to an empty room, but according to her reading, a build-up increased desire and gratification. It had.

Rachel Finds Herself...

Josh two hours into the train journey, replenished his snacks from the catering carriage, consisting of crisps and a microwaved bacon sandwich made with stale bread. Thankfully, the train had passed Milton Keynes and was on the final leg of its journey, passing through the last of the English countryside before entering London's suburbia, and finally slowing down as it continued on, passing the housing estates of Chalk Farm and Camden.

Passengers began to gather up their possessions after the intercom relayed, “We will be arriving at London Euston at 15:07. Thank you for travelling with us, we hope to see you soon.”

Josh texted Rachel.

“Back in London, can't wait to have you.”

She responded with more red heart emojis.

Rachel had spent too long soaking in the bath, but pruned herself entirely by shaving her underarms, legs, and pussy region. She was busy doing her makeup, experimenting with a different look when she received Josh's text, sending back acknowledgement with a further heart emoji. Admiring herself in the bedroom mirror, she was delighted with her new look: carefully applied eye makeup, lip gloss, a new blue minidress, and racy underwear.

She stood up, back straight, pushing her boobs out,

and having squeezed into her high heels, Rachel felt taller and more sophisticated – sexy: a feeling that had always alluded her in the past. Her groin area felt fresh and clean, but tickled erotically, sensitive to her lady shave. Dabbing Marc Jacobs perfume behind her ears and wrists, she also added a tad on her shaven region, as suggested by the internet.

She wished she had not - it stung like hell.

Josh sat back in his taxi, not enjoying the road humps and bumps. He had forgotten how old fashioned they were compared to the luxury of the Mercedes S-Class that he had got used to in Manchester.

Rachel made sure that the ice dispenser was full and checked on the chicken and roast potatoes. Supper cooked and ready at about 7:00 p.m. which left ample time to seduce her husband first. She lit the new arousal scented candles and positioned them around the living room. The marital bed was dressed in fresh ironed sheets and pillowcases.

Rachel, to keep her in the mood, needed aphrodisiacs. Sex to her in the past was only for the bedroom. Some of her reading disgusted her, and some kinky suggestions she had not even heard of. Her inner self was key, and most articles advocated as much. Rachel mixed vermouth and gin and added olives to make her first dirty dry Martini. It tasted not quite cold enough as she began sipping it seated on her patterned settee. Picking up a borrowed copy of an erotic novel she thumbed through until she found a turned in page. She began to read.

"They kissed passionately; tongues entwined as his muscled arms lifted her easily onto the kitchen granite worktop."

She let the words sink in, drinking her Martini, the warmth of the alcohol embracing her as read the novel. She was the sultry passionate character being carried into the kitchen.

Josh arrived at his small, terraced home and paid the taxi driver with no monetary tip but a verbal one, pointing out the driver's error in not driving the shortest route. The driver swore under his breath, muttering something which sounded antisemitic. Josh asked the driver to repeat what he said, but the driver ignored and U-turned in a single manoeuvre, speeding off.

He found his front door key, noting the front garden appeared to be in a better state than before he left.

Rachel beat him to it and opened the front door before he inserted his key into the lock, looking ravishing in her low-cut figure-hugging blue minidress, with matching blue high heels which Josh was sure he had not seen previously.

"Hi, darling. You look stunning."

He kissed her lips chastely. Rachel responded uncharacteristically by teasing his lower lip, using the tip of her tongue. He smelt her lightly scented perfume and tasted her fresh glossy lipstick as he followed her lead, her wet, probing tongue entering his waiting mouth, writhing uncontrollably in its deep exploration, comparable to their first passionate kiss on that long-ago second date. Josh's eyes locked with his wife's, clear and wide in their inflamed desire. She allowed him to lead, easing her head back, hot lips open and inviting, warm breath urging for more. He did not disappoint, tongues clashing in their fight for salacious supremacy. His eyes closed. She withdrew her tongue, his frantically searching for her serpent-like lust, only finding a closed mouth, shut to further examination.

"Hi Josh," she said, slinking back from their embrace. "How was it?"

He stepped forward, shutting the door with a gentle backwards kick.

"Drink?" she said before he answered her first question.

"Don't mind if do. VAT please Darlin'," he requested as he followed her through their open plan living room, admiring her wiggling bottom as she walked into the kitchen.

Rachel opened the fridge door, bending down to pick up the cold vodka bottle. Her mind was imagining itself in her book as she sensed her husband's eagerness, his breathing close by. His nose sniffed the roasting chicken supper as his cock pushed to fuck her right here and now, his mind confused by her unusual sexual signals.

As Rachel stood up, bottle in hand, Josh pulled her round to face him. Taking the bottle from her hand, he unscrewed its top, taking a swig before passing the bottle back. She, following suit, took an extra drink before placing it open on the wooden worktop beside the fridge.

"I want you now Josh, before supper."

Josh was mystified by Rachel's straight demand - it was unusual, to say the least, just like their earlier texting.

Even more unusual was when Rachel deliberately pressed her backside against his body.

"Josh, your cock feels so hard on my tuchus - I think you want me too."

Turning her head slightly, Rachel felt warm breath as his lips lightly brushed her own. Rachel's skin tingled as Josh exhaled in excitement. Her tongue, serpent-like once more, slid back and forth, swirling against his. She was sucking on it hard as if it was his penis. Hands finding each other, Rachel led, seductively stroking and imitating a hand job on his fingers.

Turning to face him, she was grinding hard and desperately into his groin, breasts hard against his heaving chest, whispering, "I want you inside me, take me."

Josh's hand responded by roughly stroking her inner thigh, finding urgency and lacy sexy underwear. Lifting her up with strong, capable arms and positioning her on the worktop, Rachel began groaning, enjoying the thrill of the moment and the warmth of the wood on her buttocks. Josh spread her legs to increasingly blistering groans and pangs of passion, delicately kissing and teasing her inner thighs, tension building with his expert caress.

Unzipping him, she was needing his cock. Josh was filling Rachel's engaged mouth with two fingers, withdrawing and easing wet fingers into her, awaiting her moist urge. Gasping in further anticipation, Rachel guided his erection into the mouth of her arousal, tightly wrapping her legs around his waist. He fondled her breasts, pinching the nipples and adding to her heightened pleasure.

"I'm almost there, Josh" she panted as he pushed deeper into her soul.

"I know, I want you to cum for me."

Josh's words pushed her over, her vagina clenching his cock, as Rachel quivered in unabating ecstasy. His tongue deep inside her mouth, he was sensing urgent tremors, ready to erupt. Rachel climaxed, sucking hard on his tongue. Josh eased her down by kissing her neck gently and passionately.

Rachel screamed, "Don't take it out, I want more, give me more!"

The words surprised them both. Josh had never heard her demand more.

Rachel, too, felt shocked by the filthy words escaping her mouth.

Josh held his erection to her demands, keeping it

inside as directed. They continued to kiss unabatingly. He was rolling her nipples between two fingers, tenderly at first, until Rachel insisted: "Harder, don't stop. Suck them!"

She was orgasming, with more intensity than the first, in three spasmodic waves as Josh ravaged her - each stronger than the last as his seed completed her erotic fulfilment.

Both were exhausted, Josh holding her firmly in his arms, face close, her neck smelling sweet. Heartbeats were becoming more regular as their bodies came down from their extensive lovemaking. Rachel reached out, grabbed, and drank from the vodka bottle as the oven alarm sounded.

The pair disentangled from each other.

"Supper's ready," Rachel proclaimed. "You deserve it. My turn to feed you." Josh enjoyed his chicken supper and complimented his wife on the scented candles and her hard work in the kitchen, grinning at his double meaning; but as usual, the chicken soup was hot water, devoid of actual chicken. He did wonder how this soup could actually be medicinal.

Rachel carefully questioned him about her family and his new expected role within the family business, mentioning Pepper Wilder, Lydia, and the Wailer. Josh calmed her by focusing on the Wailer, and inferred he found Lydia too skinny and up her own arse, unlike his princess - that's not to say fat, but just right.

Before Rachel could interrogate him further on Lydia, Josh changed tack, saying, "You wouldn't have heard, but there was a death in Pepper Wilder."

"Really? What happened?"

"Apparently one of the dancers topped themselves."

"How?"

Rachel, all ears, like many bored housewives, was a bit of a busybody when it came to death.

"I was in the bar, drinking with Gary. I was a bit two and eight, and you know what it's like when guys drink."

"Yes, go on," said Rachel, pressing for more.

"To be honest it was only when the old Bill turned up that we knew somefink was up."

"Go on," she interrupted.

"Angel, the dancer - and no, I didn't meet her but she could 'av been dancing earlier, I'm not sure, didn't really watch the dancers - anyway, Gary said she took an overdose in the changing room."

"Yeah, right, and why?"

"No idea, but I heard it was something about her boyfriend."

The conversation continued in front of the TV as they cuddled up with nosh, before eventually both needing their bed and sleep.

An Interesting First Day...

A few weeks later, after some marital alone time, Josh woke unusually early, remarkably refreshed, and ready for almost anything. His wife, as usual, was snoring - or as he called it, "snorting". He did not disturb her, showered, and dressed in his work suit, ready for his first day within the family enterprise. He kissed her goodbye on the cheek after leaving a cup of tea and toast on the bedside table.

She stirred enough to wish him luck and say, "See you later, husband."

Closing the front door quietly, he plugged the warehouse location into his Sat Nav and started the engine of his four-year-old Ford Mondeo. It did not take Josh long to arrive at the family's London warehouse, a short drive from their home in Leyton, East London.

The building was on an industrial estate just off the East India Dock Road, with one of those boards showing the names of the various businesses situated within. Josh easily found the correct building after reading the family business name on the board. According to the board, Maximillian Food Distribution was third on the right, first left. Josh pressed the intercom by the entrance barrier. It lifted automatically after a security camera seemingly scanned his vehicle. Josh parked his car in one of several bays marked "Maximillian visitors only".

Elsewhere in one of the few East London police stations still remaining, there was a buzz of activity in the open plan office which accommodated the murder squad detectives. Detective Constable Johnson had just finished reading a vehicle forensic report from an incident which took place eight weeks earlier in the Limehouse Link Tunnel. A small calibre bullet was discovered by the forensic team in the wheel arch of the victim's Ford Fiesta, a car belonging to a Miss Elizabeth Jane Moore. The deceased driver was a known small-time fence named Harry Caine who occasionally worked as a warehouse courier. His last legitimate employment was as a courier for a business on the East India Dock Industrial Estate. He was known to the police as a bit of a flash Harry, and his girlfriend Elizabeth was known to local police not through a rap sheet, but as a good fuck as she often frequented the station pub hang out. D.C. Johnson was not lucky in that department. Likely, because of his looks, women tended not to give a second glance to a middle-aged, fat, blonde constable with a receding hairline. Johnson was not a good murder detective, but often took credit for his underlings' hard work, possibly the reason why younger officers below him surpassed him in status. What he knew about Elizabeth was information gleaned from the toilet cubicle. To the department and beyond she was known as easy.

His visit to the toilet this morning implied she had

been had the night before.

As he put the report down on his untidy desk, his governor, Inspector Lemmings called the team together for this particular enquiry; it had been officially classified as a murder investigation.

Josh, on entering the warehouse, was directed to the personal office to fill out new employee paperwork by a cheerful middle-aged woman. He was directed to take a seat once in the office by a Mr. Patel, the head of HR, who was busy thumbing through files on his pristine and organised desk. Mr. Patel offered his hand, Josh shook it. He asked to be spared for a minute while he browsed through Josh's limited paperwork. Mr Patel, understanding Josh's connection, made an internal phone call.

"Mr. Levy will see you in a moment, Mr. Goldstein - and welcome to the establishment."

Inspector Lemmings enjoyed holding court. She recently transferred in from the drug squad and relished her new challenge; seven years of drug investigations fulfilled her at first, especially the last two years spent as the primary investigator, but the last eight months were a drag, taking their toll on her long-term relationship with Ann, her partner of nine years. Ann had left after too many nights and days alone. Ann decided that raising a child by herself may as well be full time, without the need of her partner Patricia.

The murder case was Inspector Patricia's first, and she intended to impress the high-ups with a quick result. She surveyed her team in front of her: four officers including the ignoramus D.C. Johnson, whose lazy reputation preceded him.

"Morning team. I hope you have all read the reports that I circulated this morning. I see, D.C. Johnson, that you have read the forensic report. I want you to visit Miss Moore, the owner of the vehicle and boyfriend of the deceased - one Harry Cain. I want you to find what she knows about Harry's connections and habits; if she knows how he came into money."

" Yes, Ma'am, understood," said D.C. Johnson.

"Can I suggest you liaise with Police Constable Sandos; but be gentle with her, it's her first death duty call."

"Of course, ma'am."

His colleagues jibed him: "Don't forget your truncheon."

"That's enough boys - and Constable Khan," the only other female officer directly involved in the case, "can you pay a visit to the food distribution warehouse, his last known employment? Detective Best can accompany you; extra eyes may be prudent."

Inspector Lemmings, after her orders, indicated

that during her time in the drug unit this warehouse was subject to an investigation about five years ago, but no charges were ever brought.

"Detective West, can you check into the old files from that case? Can I suggest you speak to D.C. Snoot who originally worked on that inquiry just in case we missed something - and West, next time I see you, I don't want to see you in yesterday's clothes - it's not befitting of the force."

"Sorry Ma'am, it won't happen again."

"That's all detectives, thank you, and keep me informed; we need to get the bastards that did this, and perhaps we will get lucky with the drugs angle."

"Yes, Ma'am," the team said in unison, getting up from their seats.

"Pleased to meet you Josh, call me Ed," Mr Levy said as he entered the small HR office. "I will show you around and then we can have a chat. Your Grandfather, Max has filled me in and speaks highly of you. I'm fully aware of your reasons for being here. I'm due to retire in the next three years and my job is to teach you about our entire business model."

Josh fully understood the implications of Ed's straight-talking. Mr. Patel did not, as he was only involved in the kosher end of the business.

Ed took Josh on a tour of the warehouse and

introduced him to only a few colleagues, those deemed necessary for his role. One aisle of the warehouse stocked tins of kosher food as well as biscuit packets. Certain sections were a mixture of legit kosher and "other". The "other" could only be seen by the light scanner Ed used to highlight an extra small white dot between some of the packaging wording.

This light scanner was a standard QR code reader, with an intelligent finger scanner concealed at the back of the code reader. Ed explained there were three of these in total. He had possession of one, and Josh, once set up, would have access to another. The third was in a small safe in the main office. Ed explained that if the non-standard finger scanner were discovered, it would fail, as it needed the user's smartphone. Josh was looking confused until Ed asked to see his mobile and explained how to use the hidden app. Both needed to be touched by the same finger within seconds to get past the QR device's subterfuge. Josh finally comprehended why he was given a new smartphone during his trip to Manchester. He asked a further question on how other staff did not collect and deliver the wrong goods. Ed showed him how that worked on a standard QR Device.

The next walkaround was in the kosher wine aisle. Josh knew about the wine and fathomed rightly the scanner was used here in a similar fashion to the tinned food.

Josh felt the cushioned floor underfoot in this area which appeared to be newly laid. He decided this must save on breakage expenses.

The Police Visit…

A van driver, having just finished a delayed delivery, watched through his centre mirror as the two officers arrived at the warehouse. At first, he did not realise they were for Maximillian Foods as they parked their police vehicle in the next-door business bay.

Josh felt the cold on the final part of the grand tour when Ed invited him into the large and well-stocked walk-in freezer, which surprised him with its ingeniousness: it held a smaller secret freezer with a passcode to gain entry. The secret unit held kosher chickens, beef, and lamb. Ed showed him stuffed chickens filled not with giblets, but cocaine, wrapped in chicken-coloured sealed bags and covered with uncleaned chicken guts. The Beef and lamb held similar in their cavities.

Detective Constable Johnson and Constable Sandos arrived at Miss Moore's home within the hour. On the journey, Johnson did try chatting up the young P.C. under the guise of helpfulness, but she saw through it and put pay to his poor effort swiftly and politely by indicating that she was in a long-term relationship. She wasn't, but he got the message and changed the subject.

"As I believe you have already met her, you can lead the questions."

"Err, no, I have not Sir, you're misinformed. But as

a woman I'm happy to lead."

He was being his usual lazy self, allowing someone else to do the work. He did not bother reading the details of Miss Moore's relationship with the deceased. His only real interest was in ogling the young lady, as he did at a distance when colleagues actually chatted to her at the station's local pub.

Miss Moore did not answer the door and on closer inspection, it was clear she had not been in for at least a couple of days, as post and takeaway leaflets hung out of the letterbox of the front door.

The food distribution van driver, on alighting his vehicle, was confronted by the two police officers. One in plain clothes and a uniformed female officer. She asked politely if they could both be shown the whereabouts of the personnel, without giving a reason.

The van driver, having a nervous stutter, eventually got the words, "Of course, officers," out, offering to take them himself.

He led them to a side door and guided them to Mr. Patel's office, as he had the good sense to know that walking them through the storage route would create idle chatter.

He knocked on Mr Patel's door.

"Two officers to see you," he announced, having difficulty in getting his words out.

"Morning officers, how can I help?"

Detective Constable Best introduced both himself and P.C. Khan. Constable Khan took out her notebook from the top pocket of her uniform and withdrew the small pencil from its centre, as D.C. Best confirmed "It's just a routine enquiry on one of your former employees."

"And the name of that person?" Mr Patel asked curtly. He hated having his work interrupted by anyone and the police were no exception.

D.C. Best responded, "A Mr. Harry Caine, one of your van drivers."

"Ah yes, easy fellow to remember: like the footballer, but the different spelling of course."

P.C. Khan smiled as she was a football fan and adored the player to the extent that her mobile phone wallpaper held his image.

Mr. Patel stood up from behind his desk. Before opening the filing cabinet, he needed to locate the small cabinet key to unlock the three draws. Checking a couple of desk draws, he mumbled "Where could it be? I had it just a moment ago."

He began to rummage his tidy desk.

D.C. Best shuffled on his feet impatiently and interrupted Mr. Patel's browsing.

"Can I use the toilet?"

"Yes, yes, of course, it's left out the door, down the corridor and the gents are just after the ladies."

"Thank you!" responded D.C. Best. "I'll leave you in the capable hands of P.C. Khan."

She gave her colleague a look as if to say "I know what you're up to."

Before directly looking at Mr. Patel, who was still hunting for the elusive key, P.C. Khan fiddled with her notebook and looked around the tidy office. She decided all was as it should be.

"Ah, found it," Mr. Patel exclaimed. "It was in my jacket." He said this while unlocking the cabinet and easily finding and retrieving the file labelled "Harry Caine, Van Driver".

He sat down back at his desk, opened the file and asked, "What do you need to know, officer?"

"Ah yes Mr. Patel. When did Mr. Caine join Maximillian? How was his conduct, as an employee? Who were his friends here?"

"Can I ask why you need that information? Didn't he die a couple of months ago in a car accident?"

P.C. Khan referred to her notebook before saying, "It's now an enquiry."

"Ah, into the accident?" said Mr. Patel.

"No Sir, between you and me it's now a murder investigation - but I haven't told you that."

Mr. Patel was picking up a hint of a Bangladeshi accent within her cockney sounding voice. He turned a couple of pages before stating that he, Mr. Caine, joined the business eighteen months ago, late only once. He suffered two slight accidents in the company van, but always reported them as per company policy."

P.C. Khan made a note of Mr. Caine's start date and added two slight RTAs. Her ears pricked up when Mr. Patel explained a slight commotion in the kosher wine section of the warehouse after Mr. Caine clumsily broke a crate of wine bottles, which led to harsh words. According to Mr. Patel, that took place a few weeks before the car crash.

Ed, while having a general chat with Josh, spotted a suited character that he had not seen before toying with goods stacked on their shelves. He shouted loudly across to the person.

"Oi, what are you doing? You don't work here."

D.C. Best looked up and said the first thing that entered his head.

"Can I buy these? My wife loves gherkins."

Ed now beside him, with Josh watching, responded in an angered tone: "Err, no, this is not a supermarket for the public - we are strictly wholesale only. How did you get in?"

The detective had little choice but to admit who he was by waving his warrant card at Ed and asserted, "Sorry, Sir, I couldn't resist, I got lost coming back from the toilet. I'm actually with Mr. Patel."

"Are you? We'd better take you back, hadn't we - we

don't want the Met's finest on the missing list. This is a trained-staff-only area. We, at all times, follow and adhere to health and safety guidelines. I suggest you follow me to Mr. Patel's Office."

Ed made a point of closely inspecting the warrant card before leading the officer back to the personnel office.

D.C. Best followed him back meekly after patting his cheap off-the-peg polyester suit jacket down. He had found something of possible interest.

Josh smirked intentionally as all three walked at a pace to Mr. Patel's office.

P.C. Khan had noted all as required and was having general football chit-chat whilst drinking tea with Mr. Patel as her colleague returned from his walkabout. She had found Mr. Patel very affable, which was her final note in her police notepad before returning it to her pocket. Ed could not resist a final dig at her colleague's expense.

"I believe he's one of yours. I assume he's never worked traffic as he claimed to have gotten lost after using the lavatory."

P.C. Khan looked Ed up and down, noting the Tottenham cockerel tattoo on his left muscled arm and his wide heaving chest. She was forced to grin and could not resist the chance to belittle the experienced detective.

"Yes, he's one of ours. He's always wandering off and getting himself lost." D.C. Best grimaced and confirmed she had completed their initial enquiry.

"Thank you for your time and valuable help. If it's okay, we will return if we require more," Best said, looking embarrassed.

"My pleasure officers, anytime. Here's my business card. Ed, can you show them both out and give the officers your card just in case it's required?"

Ed only handed the attractive constable his business card, claiming it was his last one after catching her sustained second glance at him - because he knew it would further piss off the plain-clothed detective.

Back in the police car, D.C. Best produced his discovery.

"What do you think of this?" he said as he waved what appeared to be part of a punt under P.C. Khan's nose.

She looked at it without touching and replied back as she opened a passenger glove box in front of her.

"Don't look much to me - it's a shard of dark glass. What's that about?"

"A punt, or dimple is what you call the bottom of a wine bottle. I'm sure you're familiar with that."

P.C. Khan in her head thought, "What an arse, he has put his mitts all over it." She stayed professional and handed him a small clear evidence bag.

"Put it in here and we will take it to the lab back at the station, perhaps we will get lucky."

She took out her notebook and added, "Found in the warehouse, without specifics, possibly a punt."

Her comrade handed it back to her in its evidence bag with a grunt and started the engine of the pooled police vehicle. During the drive back, Best thought of promotion - “I've cracked the case”.

Khan thought, “Maybe I will give that Ed a call tonight, he's a bit of alright. He can give me one anytime he likes.”

Josh followed Ed to a small discreet office, which housed not much more than a desk, a telephone, computer, and some old wall-framed black and white photos of who he assumed was a young Max along with others outside a small shop front with the store name Maximillian Kosher Food. Ed confirmed what Josh already thought: that this was his office. He also informed Josh his first business appointment was with an elderly rabbi and son due in at 2:00 p.m. Josh remembered that these two were the kosher inspectors, as he put it, who were discussed up north. Neither of them mentioned the police visit as both decided it was a standard enquiry.

Ed, before leaving him to get acquainted with his new surroundings, handed him a gold company credit card, complete with the familiar Pepper Wilder emblem, and a VIP membership card for Pepper Wilder 2. Ed explained this gave full access to the gentleman’s club and guaranteed on-the-spot reservations at the family’s two London-based restaurants - the details of all were listed on the reverse of the membership card.

Josh, after Ed left, phoned the bar/restaurant simply named "74 Joes" and booked a table for two that evening. After booking he telephoned Rachel, saying in an enthusiastic voice, "You deserve a good night out - will up west do?"

Rachel was glad her husband telephoned and looked forward to their date together. She understood that her sexual prowess over the last few weeks was the instigator of their newfound closeness and that maybe she was ready to visit Pepper Wilder 2 for the first time.

The last two weeks were the happiest she had felt for a long time. Josh was attentive and patient as they experimented sexually and Rachel felt liberated, as if shackles of her past had been removed. Josh had suggested her mental block must have come from early sexual experiences that somehow damaged her sexual fulfilment. Rachel deep down knew he was right, especially as it was her that kept advancing their sexual exploration.

They had visited the family restaurant previously, but never as a couple, and tonight she intended to push boundaries further.

As the two officers arrived back at the nick, Best took hold of the potential evidence as after all, he had found it and always liked a pat on the back. He recently arrested an East End serial killer which had gone national due to the killer's preference for biting penises off of his young victims and cooking the phallus as a romantic meal with various female dates. The Phallus Valentine killer was *the* tabloid press front page headline. He was trapped when he unintentionally dated a female police officer who realised she was eating something odd and human in texture. She took her findings to D.C. Best, as he was the contact officer leading the case, and he took great pride in the arrest a few weeks later. The press was spoon-fed information over a two-week period, suggesting that it was actual police work that netted the killer, not luck.

After a discussion with Inspector Patricia Lemmings, who voiced her doubts about the punt having any value as it was ostensibly obtained illegally, however, understanding its potential, she decided to have it sent to the police laboratory for forensic testing.

"We will get around it, should it highlight something of interest."

Several hours later, Josh completed a successful first business meeting with the elderly rabbi and son, with the son suggesting the two take a taxi to Pepper Wilder 2 for the mid-afternoon show.

Sexual Banter & Date Night...

Josh telephoned Rachel en route.

"Hi gorgeous. It looks like my meeting is going on longer than I'd planned. Do you mind if we meet at the bar, at Joes?"

"Yes, that's fine Josh, but can we play that game we discussed last week? It might be fun."

"Of course, darling." Josh knew what she meant, her other recent games always leading to erotic sex.

Rachel named her game "Pick Me Up at the Bar", having stolen the idea from her constant internet reading over the last few weeks and finding, for the first time in her life, that she actually enjoyed sex, especially some of their experimenting. They had even gone into a mainstream high street sex shop and purchased a soft porn movie together to watch cuddled up on their sofa.

Josh behaved himself at Pepper Wilder 2, finding it very similar in design and ambience to its bigger sister. One pole dancer reminded him of Lydia, and while the rabbi's son enjoyed a private dance, he sent a text message to her. She responded promptly with an explicit image and the words, "Missing this?"

He sent an image back of the look-alike Lydia wording it, "Not quite, I'm with this!"

Her response was more explicit.

"Does she play with you like me?"

Josh knew she was fishing and sent, "I'll let you know."

Their banter continued on in the same vein, with Lydia becoming more intense and pornographic in her wording and images, including stills of their threesome. Josh, however, was finding it difficult to keep up as Rachel, too, was sending him messages, although not as blatant in their sexual overtones. For safety's sake, he relayed to Lydia an upcoming business meeting in Manchester and, as she insisted, he would fuck her then.

Josh deleted Lydia's sexting, ramping the banter up with Rachel who did likewise to the extent that she was in a taxi on the way to a date and asked, "Do you think my date will like this?" after sending an image of her knickerless crotch.

P.C. Khan was also texting while at home alone, deciding tonight she needed some fun, and the thought of having Ed's muscular, firm body prompted her initial text to Ed.

"Do you want to buy me dinner tonight?"

Ed was still at work when he received this surprising text and said "Sure" after realising it was from that rather attractive policewoman. A text came back.

"Why not? You decide the venue, but no earlier than 9 as I don't finish until 8."

P.C. Khan was happy and nervous at the same time

as she had not been on a date for months. She sent a final text back to Ed using her first name, Kayra, in confirmation of their first date.

Hot Dates...

Rachel took in her surroundings while seated in a discreet corner of the restaurant bar after arriving thirty minutes early, ordering a dirty dry martini.

It was her first visit to 74 Joes since its refit six months ago. Her family had invited them both to the grand opening but unfortunately, they could not attend as Josh's side of the family suffered a bereavement - an elderly aunt - and Rachel, being a dutiful Jewish wife, did the right thing by supplying constant tea and bagels to the bereaved attendees.

She was feeling excited and not out of place in the opulent modern decor of the revamp. The space behind the stick was mirrored with a blue blacklight which shimmered on the array of alcoholic beverages, each in their own spot. Every shelf was housing a particular premium spirit. The four bartenders were dressed immaculately in three-piece suits, with the only female dressed similarly but wearing a skirt.

Rachel too was dressed in a black skirt, giving just enough freedom of movement when she took her seat. Her skirt was matching her satin silk buttoned shirt and she thought "perfect" as she admired her image in the bar's mirror.

She sipped at her just-right Martini as she felt a tap on her shoulder.

Kayra, in a not so salubrious part of town, was also at a bar, but sitting behind a restaurant table sipping a cold lager, perusing the bar menu while waiting for her first date. She was dressed in her favourite high-waisted black faux leather trousers and white crop top showing her pierced navel adorned with a gold closure ring. She, too, was excited, and already decided that if Ed and she hit it off, it was back to her place for sex as she has been too long without cock.

Rachel turned elegantly, half expecting Josh. It was not.

"Can I buy you a drink?" said the smooth sounding voice.

Looking him up and down, she found him a rather handsome man with deep, engaging blue eyes intently staring at her.

A rush of excitement shot through her.

"I'm sorry, I'm waiting for my date."

"I half expected that," said the stranger hitting on her.

"But... if he has the audacity to let a beautiful lady down, I implore you, do come and find me."

Rachel giggled and glowed with the impertinence and dialogue the stranger used. The stranger, being a gentleman, took his leave as he put it, leaving Rachel to her drink. She drank the remainder of her Martini, ordering a second.

Kayra watched as Ed sauntered over to her table. He was confident in his walk with its swagger. She liked that in a man. He looked like the perfect hunk in his tight white t-shirt and equally tight jeans, perfectly highlighting his bulge between his legs, giving her widest smile as he lightly kissed both cheeks in a continental fashion sitting down opposite her.

"Another drink, Kayra? - Have I pronounced your name right?"

She again liked that in a man. It showed caring and thoughtfulness.

"Yes, perfect. It means 'gift of God'. And yes, please can I have another?" She pointed at her near-empty glass. Kayra liked to point that out to a promising date to gauge their response.

Ed looked up to the high roof pub ceiling and exclaimed, "Thank you, God, for providing me with such a wonderful date," clasping his hands together as if in prayer.

"Not heard that one before. I like a man that's open with compliments and says what he feels."

"It's true, Kayra. Sometimes it scares the fairer sex off. I'm glad you're still sitting here and not running off to take an urgent call and making excuses to leave," Ed said, picking up the other bar menu and scanning its contents.

After a minute's hush, he asserted, "Lamb chops and mash sounds good."

Laughing, Kayra, said "'Baa, baa, meh', like that you mean?"

Ed looked up slightly perplexed as he watched her mouth change shape, and she reverted back to English. "Yeah, people always say that. They read a menu and often say it sounds good or nice. How can it? They're words, not music; menus don't hiss or sizzle."

Ed still watched her mouth as her top lip raised itself involuntarily as she said "sizzle".

Kayra liked the fact that he was watching her lips moving and not her breasts in the tight top.

"Good point," he said. "I've never thought about it before, but you're right."

At that point, a server appeared, both at first not glimpsing the waiter.

"Are you ready to order Sir? Madam?"

They both answered jointly.

"Lamb chops and mash, and tomato soup to start, please."

"I'll have a lager and my friend will have the same," Ed said as the waiter wrote down their food order.

"Salad on the side?" he offered.

Kayra interjected, "Yes please - a bit on the side is always healthy enough for two."

She glanced at Ed as she made her cheeky remark, her hand fleetingly stroking down her top. The waiter left them as Ed watched her hand, which was Kayra's intention.

Rachel Flirts with a Hot Date...

Rachel was feeling slightly tipsy as she drank the last of her cocktail.

"Is this seat taken?" said a familiar voice.

She looked up into the eyes of her husband.

"Not sure, wanna buy me a drink while I think about it?"

Josh, for an instant, held her gaze, smiling. Looking at her cocktail glass, empty apart from a remaining olive, he said, "Martini, is it? But what type?"

"Dirty and dry; the dirtier the better," she said as the already drunk spirits engulfed her.

Josh signalled a barman who immediately began to prepare Rachel's cocktail.

"I'll have a whisky sour on the rocks."

He deliberately ignored his wife's smutty comment as he glanced from the barman to her, again holding her gaze but this time a tad longer. Josh attempted to sit on the bar stool beside his wife.

"Don't think," she said, "this seat is available."

She turned on her seat as she said this, allowing Josh a glimpse of her cleavage. Josh stayed upright looking down at her breasts as she intended.

"Your titties make your bum look smaller," as he took her body in. Rachel, from her reading, understood what a compliment-insult was and reacted the way she had read to.

"You may take a seat. You can call me Rachel, and you are?" She flicked her hair back, crossing her legs as Josh broke eye contact, instead staring as her legs changed position.

Rachel felt horny in the empowerment her body had brought. The barman she secretly craved positioned two white fresh mats down, placing their drinks on top.

Josh, more sincerely than usual, thanked him for serving them both.

"I like a man with good manners, please sit. I did say it was alright to and you are."

Rachel deliberately stroked his leg with hers as he sat saying, "I see sir dresses to the left."

Josh liked his wife's game of flirtation. She had become some sort of sex goddess in the last few weeks. He was still not sure why.

"Hey, Rachel, I'm Josh. Good to meet you."

Rachel nodded, drinking from her fresh glass before placing the cocktail glass back on the bar mat, leaning forward slightly, whispering into his ear with her hand on his upper leg.

"Guess what?"

Josh gave her a thoughtful look and answered.

"I guess you want me to buy you dinner."

"Yes, that will be delicious - but it's not what I was going to say." She said this still whispering, and added,

"Do you want to buy a girl dinner that's not wearing any knickers?" giving his balls a discreet light squeeze.

"I don't believe you; can you show me?"

Rachel answered, "I can hardly lift my skirt, but does this prove it?" With that she roughly grabbed Josh's hand, swung the bar stall to a discreet position and slipped his hand up her skirt.

"Wow, I believe you," he whispered, after discovering her moist pink pearl, and being Josh, he was obliged to touch her intimately.

Rachel took a sharp intake of breath at his touch and moaned in excitement, grinding against a finger.

"Josh you can't, not here!" widening her legs to his touch.

The barman seemingly heard her groans and came over.

"Everything okay, miss? Can I you get another?"

He could not actually see their discreet activity but presumed what they were up to.

"Yes please, same again," said Josh, his fingers still exploring with Rachel doing her best not to grind.

The barman turned away to prepare their drinks as Rachel pushed her groin forward not being able to cope with the demands of her pussy.

The round of drinks arrived.

Josh was looking at his hot date as he removed his hand to her groans of displeasure. Rachel, aching for more, knew she would have to wait until later and lifted her drink to her lips, gulping half the martini down and placing it back on the table.

"Do you mind, I need to powder my nose?"

Josh nodded, looking directly at her as he stirred his whisky sour with his finger. Rachel giggled as she drank the remainder of her cocktail before stepping off her seat carefully and wandering off to the restroom, ensuring Josh got an eyeful of her wiggling arse.

The game of "Pick Me Up" was going perfectly. Knowing the barman had likely glimpsed their game added to her arousal.

Josh continued with his whisky, enjoying the moment, and contemplated on his wife's strange but welcome behaviour.

Rachel, over the last two weeks, had opened up to him sexually, allowing their lovemaking in every room of the house, including a night of passion in the back garden. He wondered if she was secretly visiting one of those sex shrinks, not that it bothered him if this continued. He dropped his local mistress after returning from Manchester. In reality, he did not need the extras she offered, as Rachel for, whatever reason, was obliging all his needs.

Josh finished his drink and requested the tab.

After paying, the over-attentive barman said, "Your table's ready. Joan, your waitress, will show you to your table."

Josh finished his whisky, excited about the evening ahead as he followed Joan to their table. Rachel was clearly in an aroused state when she left for the ladies. He was looking forward to what followed their meal.

An Off-Duty Officer Plays...

Ed and Kayra enjoyed each other's company within the throng of a busier than usual Monday night pub. The main bar was packed to the rafters as Chelsea were playing West Ham, who, unusually, with their current form, were winning.

The couple, both Spurs fans and season ticket holders, actually held tickets in the same section, thirty-three rows from each other. Ed was a proud member of the exclusive 1882 club and happily explained the extra benefits. He suggested Kayra could one day be his guest and enjoy the private bar and pre-match food. Kayra jumped at this prospect, pushing Ed as to when.

The soup arrived as shouts of "penalty" erupted from the main bar. Both listened intently to the outcome, which came three minutes later after a long VAR check. "Goal" followed by "We are forever blowing bubbles" made it clear who the likely victors would be. Four minutes later, a huge roar filled the whole establishment as the final whistle blew. As both were from the East End, both favoured West Ham over Chelsea and, after finishing their soup, discussed this at length, with Kayra consciously flirting with Ed who was a little embarrassed.

She increased her flirtation by turning to light erotic questioning, as she needed Ed's cock. His older age was not an issue. He was obviously fit and available.

"If you were a girl, which footballer would you fuck?"

"It's never crossed my mind."

Their main course arrived with the server nearly dropping the plates as the small contingent of bad-tempered Chelsea fans ran from the main bar into the restaurant end of the pub, followed by a larger contingent of West Ham fans jubilant in celebration.

Ed quipped, "Typical Chelski, always running."

Both laughed together at his quip.

Kayra, said, "Go on, who's your man crush?"

"Never thought about it, who would you like it to be?"

"Easy", she said. "Dele Alli - and Jermaine Jenas, he's very smooth lookin'."

"What both at once?"

"Yeah, me as the meat in their sandwich could be fun. But tonight, you'll do, unless you fancy being bread and I'll invite our waiter?"

Ed began coughing as he did not expect such directness from a first date, looking at her directly and observing that her lips appeared to be swollen and deeper in colour, a clear sign of arousal.

He elected to hurry their conversation, as it was clear as day she was "up for it", at least at this precise moment. He was not going to let that go to waste.

The food area had ceased taking orders and, except

for four tables spaced around the restaurant, the randy couple were almost alone in their own bubble. The main bar, relatively quiet, gave Ed a realistic reasoning process on how not to fuck it up.

"Kayra, isn't having a threesome some form of fetish?" Ed asked, laughing between a mouthful of mash.

"Don't know, is it? What seems like a fetish to one is another's arena surely," she responded.

She changed tack.

"Why did you call me? Was it my police uniform? Have you ever shagged a police officer, or do you simply want to take down my particulars?"

"No, it was your eyes, you couldn't keep them off me, so I thought, 'she's attractive and likes my appearance, might as well find out'. Certainly it was mutual, or we wouldn't be sitting here now."

"True," she said, "you are well built, in all areas, attractive, and I have an itch to scratch. I have used one of those hook-up apps occasionally, but only met two in the last year. I don't like to lie. It seems the moment you say 'police' they run for the hills."

"Oh, you mean I'm a one-night stand?"

"Well, I like to start there. What's the point if we are not a compatible shag? I lose interest." Kayra said this while rubbing his inner thigh with her foot.

Ed reacted by doing the same under the table, reaching across the table, taking her hand, stroking it gently at first in a circular motion, her fingers stretching out in appreciation. Kayra liked it, as her womanhood ignited excitedly. Both blanked out the pub surroundings, focusing on each other, as free hands forked food into mouths, each mouthful additional and infectious in the appetite for each other. The conversation turning from light erotica to pornographic, each were captivated in the other's words and body language.

Kayra knew what she wanted and intended to get it tonight.

“Ed, you wanna fuck me tonight, or just tease a girl who needs a shag?”

By now, Ed had lost his embarrassment and replied, “Yeah, I’ll fuck you hard.”

“How hard?” Her body's needs were forcing the words out of her mouth, provoking her body to lean in towards Ed. Ed leaned in as her mouth opened in expectation of their first kiss. It was sensually hard and breathy, no lip-biting, just his tongue invading her mouth. Kayra desired this, allowing it to explore, hers rapidly stroking and flicking at his.

Their passionate kiss was interrupted by the waiter.

“Ahem, can I take your plates?”

The interruption brought a stop to their mouths’ mutual foray.

“Err, yes. Can I have the bill please?” mumbled a slightly breathless Ed.

"Of course, Sir."

"Is your car here, Ed? Mine is," Kayra asked.

"It's in the car park."

"Your car or mine?"

Ed looked at her in a confused lust.

She answered for him in a wispy, breathless voice, her lips moist in the prospect of what was to come.

"I need you to shag me hard and now. You said you want to. Let's do it in my car." Her foot under the table toyed with his trouser-imprisoned cock. Its hardness told her he craved her.

"The bill, Sir," the waiter said, as he left it for the couple to peruse. He was in no mood to wait for it by their table. Experience told him they would not hang about. Ed pulled a bundle of notes from his jeans as he glanced hastily at the presented bill. He peeled the correct notes from the bundle, depositing it on the plastic tray left by the waiter. Kayra added a tip from her backpack after retrieving it from behind the chair.

"And now, Ed, for afters!"

Standing up from her seat, taking Ed's warm, large hand in hers, she manipulated him towards the establishment's car park and began whispering constant erotic demands as they walked.

"Is your package long, thick and hard? I've always preferred thick batons, especially when it slides in and out of my mouth, reaching the back of my throat." Kayra inhaled the warm night air as she resumed spilling erotic filth into Ed's ear. "I'm primal. I need my holes to be stretched."

Ed's dick was hard with her rousing narrative. In actuality, he was not used to sexual words from a woman unless during sex, but hell if this bird wants to talk dirty, why the hell not?

Her words stopped as she rummaged in her rucksack for her car keys. Ed said, without commenting on her innuendo, "Car keys, good - you found them."

Kayra turned, facing him, bent down and spoke directly to his prominent bulge.

"Better get you into my car, Mr. Bulge, looks like you wanna come out and play with me." She patted between his legs, coughed and in a gruff male impersonation said, "Yes, miss. Please, miss. Please play with me and my pal, Mr. Balls... Can you say that again? I didn't hear you. Are you shy, Mr Bulge, like your boss?" as she rubbed her ear over his trouser clad bulge.

She stood up, giggling.

It had the desired impact as Ed, laughing, clutched her firm behind, pulling her body into his. Kayra reacted in taking his face in her hands, licking her lips salaciously in yearning.

"Is this shy, Kayra?" as he obligingly brought her mouth to his.

Lips locked. Kayra ran her tongue across his lips,

breathing in his smell - a mixture of shaving cream and male testosterone. His mouth opened to her tongue's probing. She gasped at the stiffness in his jeans, running a finger across its length and guessing there were at least eight inches of available tasty beef.

Kayra pushed his body into her car's side door. The metal of her VW saloon began creaking under the strain of two bodies falling and heaving against it. Ed's hands were firm on her buttocks, as mouths fought for supremacy. His mouth was defeated as it succumbed to her tongue's penetration. Her hands inside his t-shirt were discovering a warm, deep, hairy, beating chest. Her faux leather knickers were beginning to pool with arousal, helped with eight inches of firm cock pushing on her pubic bone.

Kayra, keeping control of their French kissing, sucked hard on his tongue. A hand brushing a recently shaved face relished the sensation of smoothness. Distant music was playing close enough to recognise the tune, deep smooching to the beat of the distant drum.

Ed's hand was tracing the contours of her firm midriff, finding her gold closure ring, playfully tugging at it as they continued to passionately embrace.

Kayra guided his hand to her trouser zip, and taking the hint, Ed slid it down, Kayra encouraging fingers to play over moist knickers, breathing heavily, sucking just a little too hard on his tongue. He jerked back in reaction, the back of his head catching the pillar of the car door's window. Kayra chuckled at his misfortune, patting the back of his head, announcing, "There, there, what shall we do to make it better?"

Again, taking his hand in hers, she was leading him to the other side of the VW parked in the last space, partially hidden by several trees and a brick wall. Eight inches of cock were available. Kayra badly craved it and did not want any disturbance to distract them.

Ed was too much of a gentleman to force, even with the earlier blatant whispered hints.

Kayra always enjoyed giving head outside a car, fresh air always adding intensity and prolonged desire for later car shagging. A near nine-inch cock, if available, was a temptation not to be overlooked.

Hidden from view, the couple snuggled and resumed their caressing slowly, intentionally basking in the build-up of desired sexual chemistry. Kayra, needing more, took the lead, unfastening his jeans. Ed eased himself against the car in expectation as she carefully withdrew his engaged cock from his jeans, the shyness of his large member temporally gone.

It was a childhood thing, often prevalent as a schoolboy being bullied by both older boys and girls; girls who could be so cruel they would show him their tits for a peek at his oversized member, then running off laughing, his embarrassment particularly nasty during sports lessons. It was only later as a football player for the college league that he understood his asset's worth. The rumours were nonetheless there but created a need for discovery amongst the girls when wearing tight football shorts. Blowjobs became the norm.

Kayra stroked his cock slowly at first, admiring its girth, standing back initially for a full aesthetic view. It drove her excitement as she dropped to her knees, scraping loose gravel on the parking surface. She was looking up into Ed's eyes, clear and focused on their oral quest. Close up, the length and thickness appeared even larger, perhaps nearer nine inches, thought Kayra.

Some dealing with a cock that size would flinch, but not her. It helped that she did not have a gag reflex. Kayra intended to take her time with her trophy, as she had to confess this was the first time she was going to fuck and suck on such a large, thick member. She fixed her eyes on Ed, flicking his rod with her tongue, serpent-like at first, Ed watching intently as she performed a similar task on his ballbag but stroking lighter. The music was still playing, softer now, more of a tap- tap-tap and ...tap. as she returned to flicking in time with the sound in her ears.

Ed attempted to ram himself into her mouth, Kayra pulling back, teasing, fingering her navel ringlet.

"Not yet, Mr. Bulge. Patience comes to those that wait."

Ed felt her warm breath on his cock as she spoke,

his urge to fill her mouth difficult to sustain. Her eyes were piercing in teasing merriment.

Kayra, in complete self-control, continued and murmured "Mr. Bulge, we have to start again."

Unfortunately for Ed, the distant melody sped up. Kayra chuckled at this as she flicked her tongue faster in and out, finally brushing his glistening tip, tasting its seeping head. Her self-control was waning at the mere flavour and aroma. Fingers slipped from her navel to her accessible groin, touching and finding saturated moisture. Ed's jutting cock continued to trickle, compelling her to withdraw fingers and finally concentrate on his magnificent sausage. Kayra, using both hands, stroked up and down slowly licking the head, exhaling warm breath over his tip and shaft. Her gaze still fixed on Ed, she lapped his entire length, varying the tempo and momentum.

Now was the moment of truth: could she take it all in? Withdrawing her mouth, sucking hard at the tip as his body motion urged for head, devouring inch by inch as it pushed towards the back of her throat. Expert hands were controlling the speed of his thrusting, Ed groaning as it finally hit the back of her throat. Kayra held it there, massaging it with her grateful tongue, seeing it almost as a challenge not to gag - never a problem with previous partners, but this was her biggest. It was exhilarating and a huge turn on. Ed's thrusting increased as she allowed him to slide in and out, pushing further into the back of her deep throat. She wanted him to come but hoped he had enough to plunge her pussy later.

Ed's eyes glazed, watching his member stretching her enthusiastic mouth as she feasted greedily.

Kayra was sure his cock was getting thicker as it approached trigger point. It began to surge as she deepthroated him.

Finally, his groin propelled all nine inches of meat into her as he flooded the back of her throat with warm, thick cum. It throbbed and streamed as she swallowed and drank. Kayra, exhilarating in her skill, allowed him to keep it deep as the stream slowed to a trickle. Her dream of a large nine-inch cock filling her mouth with cum was always on her bucket list, knowing the instant the cock was inside her pussy she too would explode. Ed finally withdrew, still hard. Kayra could not resist a final hard suck on the head for the leftover trickle, swallowing, relishing the subtle taste as he watched her drink.

Kayra gradually stood up, knees aching due to the prolonged contact with the loose gravel surface. Wiping the stickiness off from around her mouth with her forearm, she was excited that it was only residue as most of it was inside her. She smiled at Ed; face muscles strained from their endeavour. He stood there exposed; nine inches semi-hard, saliva and cum shimmering in the ambient light.

"Thank you, Mr. Bulge, for stretching my mouth. I

hope you have enough energy to stretch my snatch." she announced in her sluttiest tone. Turning her gaze to Ed, she continued, "I think, Mr. Bulge, that Ed, your boss deserves a smoke. I'll put you away for later."

With that she zipped Mr. Bulge up and removed a packet of cigarettes from her car's glove box.

Ed accepted her offer of a smoke, took two from the box, lit both and handed Kayra one.

"Such a gentleman," she said, deeply inhaling, enjoying the flavour.

Kayra and Ed did not have that much to say to each other; she was not sure if that was because he was embarrassed or that, other than sex and football, they were not compatible on much else. Kayra, however, still wanted him for obvious reasons.

"Fuckbuddies" is how she decided their relationship could evolve in the future. Ed, she figured, would want more, but she really could not see it. He had streetwise intelligence, but not much else. She could hardly picture visits to the opera or him fitting in with her friendship circle. His donkey-size dick would create attention amongst some, but most would see him as a boring late-1980s leftover.

Fuckbuddy will do then.

Dropping her finished cigarette onto the gravel and for the first time since they left the pub, she heard the rustle of the trees close by and not much else.

"Ed, you put your brains on that?" pointing to her dog-end flickering in the gravel.

Ed obliged and ground the butt into the grit with the sole of his trainers.

"Fancy a drive?" he said, his first words since the blowjob.

Ed needed another half hour at least to recover from her extraordinary oral skills. He liked the way she looked and carried herself, but not her chitchat. He had met her sort before; not the police sort, but he always felt slightly nervous around women who owned their sexuality. He was not against it, but he was just not used to it. Kayra clearly was sexually frustrated, and his penis was the reason she wanted to fuck. He was a bit old-fashioned like that. He preferred several dates first before intercourse. He was her trophy and knew what was to come, obliging her again - as how could he not. Most women ran a mile when they saw his size, but not so-called "size queens" who got off on big dicks.

"Good idea," agreed Kayra, "I know a nice quiet spot where we won't be disturbed, I want you all to myself." She was a little frustrated as her cock-sucking had already brought her close. It always did.

Eight inches filling her would be a perfect end to the evening and her recent lack of fulfilment, especially with a little inducement on her part.

Car Play...

Kayra drove out the car park and turned left in an easterly direction.

Ed seated in the passenger seat asked, “Where are we off to?”

“It’s not far - it’s a car park on one of those outdoor retail shopping places, it's nice and quiet.” She did think of driving back to her place, but her bucket list of car park intercourse needed to be ticked off. Unbeknownst to Ed, Kayra was part of a group of single police servicewomen who met once a month like a book club, but their group was called “Any Time, Any Place!” It meant what it said on the tin. Kayra lagged behind due to her lack of dates and tonight was already achieving bonus points because of his size. The group always required evidence; her car dash cam covered that. Over drinks conquest footage was used and scored on merit after a vote. There were rules:

1. Only the owner of the footage could share to the group if happy to do so.

2. Anyone sharing without permission was banned.

3. Permission from the partner must be shown as true.

4. The club is secret and new members can only be nominated by current or previous members, provided they are in the police service.

"Oh, ok." he replied. He had rather hoped to go back to her place. He looked around the car: it was spotless and clutter-free. Noticing the car dashcam, he asked, "Was that on earlier?" He knew the answer, the thought of it at first worried him and, with no unexpected justification, he felt his hardness growing back to life.

"Yes, of course. Don't want my car broken into, is that ok? I can delete it if you want."

"No need. I have to admit, it's a bit of a turn-on knowing."

Kayra took her left hand off the steering wheel and felt between his legs, finding his erect manhood.

"Yes, I can feel that," she said. "Glad, you approve."

Her hand was sending the caress to her brain, which sent a brazen signal to her already desperate and flooded pussy. Reacting to her own needs, she slid her hand from his warm crotch to her breasts, squeezing and cupping, sending further waves of erotic passion to her sensitive clit.

Ed watched as she focused on herself before he positioned a hand between her legs, stroking thighs, creating an instant moan of further arousal from Kayra. Moving her hand onto his, she began directing it firmly onto her vagina as she massaged herself over faux leather. Driving became slightly hazardous as Kayra rocked backwards and forwards in her seat with their hands' movements, especially as from the corner of her eye she could see Ed was touching himself as he worked her into a frenzy.

"Shit!" Kayla exclaimed.

"What's wrong?" Ed thought he had hurt her in some way, sending his dick back down to five inches.

"It's the police. What speed was I doing? How much have we drunk?"

"Err, fuck," he said as he turned and looked at the vehicle behind. Sure enough, it was a police car. It was not showing a blue light, but the driver was flashing the car's headlights. Kayla slowed her car down and pulled up roughly a quarter of a mile from where she initially saw the police. Images of failing the breath test and losing her job as a policewoman flashed through her mind. She felt her body heat up, different from a few minutes earlier, when it was in lust, looking around at Ed, who appeared to be calm and collected.

Well, she decided he was not driving.

The police car stopped close behind with its strong strobe light, filling her car with its beam. Kayra knew the form. The occupants were checking to see how many people were in her car and looking for conscious signs of panic. Steadying her breathing, turning the car ignition off after pressing the window switch to lower it, she prepared for the imminent arrival of the officers. The glare prevented her from seeing them leave the car properly, but experience told her there were two officers, knowing one would hold back and observe the proceedings, the other explaining the reason for the stop.

Ed and Kayra simultaneously zipped themselves back up as she caught a glimpse in the driver's wing-mirror of a male policeman approaching.

"Good evening, madam, have you been drinking tonight? You appeared to be driving rather erratically."

"Evening officer. I had two beers a few hours ago with my friend."

"I can smell alcohol on your breath madam, I will have to breathalyse you."

"Of course, officer."

Kayra hoped her speech wasn't slurred and made a point of speaking correctly in concise English.

The officer produced the breathalyser and asked her politely to step out of the vehicle. As expected, Kayra obliged, and as she opened her car door, noted the other officer, a female, reach for her police radio.

A moment later, a voice she recognised shrieked, "Kayra, is that you?!"

Kayra turned, as did the young constable beside her. As luck would have it, the shriek belonged to a buddy, one of her club circle.

"Off you pop," her mate instructed her colleague. "I will deal with this, she's an officer at my old station." The inexperienced officer did as instructed after thanking Kayra for complying with his instruction.

Kayra's police friend, now beside her, pulled out her breathalyser as a show of intent to the young officer having decided Kayra was not over the limit: in fact, she guessed why not when she glimpsed the chiselled face of Ed and his massive arms.

Kayra relaxed as they chatted. Ed could hear bits of the conversation, such as "ten points", "stretched", "I would" and "fuck", understanding that the officer must at least be a friend. The girls chatted for a few more minutes with Ed getting the distinct impression they were discussing the size of his manhood and the blowjob, made noticeable as Kayra's friend illustrated by sucking and stroking the breathalyser equipment as she fixed her eyes on him. Ed found this incredibly titillating in an experience that he had not felt before.

Kayra hugged her friend goodbye and returned to her car smiling and exclaimed in her husky voice, "I'm horny for you Ed, I want you. Is it growing?"

It certainly was, Ed was stiff with enthusiasm, especially with the help of his little blue friend, Viagra - he had slyly digested one before they set off. She made an extreme sexual proposal. Ed liked the idea but even with the Viagra, in all honesty, he was not sure if he could manage it.

Fifteen minutes later, in the seclusion of the large, empty supermarket car park, lit up only by the brightness of the full moon, Kayra was sitting astride Ed, both in their top clothing but little else. Ed was touching her swollen breasts under her crop top, her skimpy bra dispensed with on the driver's seat. Her hands started slowly running over his thick hair and down his large broad shoulders; she was adoring the feel of a strong male body pressed firmly against hers. Eight inches of man meat was close to her entrance, teasing its clit into submission, her inner lips salivating in an effort to clench his throbbing length. They kissed as hand movements switched constantly, each hand finding and exploring new, unknown erogenous zones.

Ed's mouth switched to focus on her breasts, licking and encircling but avoiding her nipples. Kayra was gasping in intensity, urging his tongue to reach her areola, eventually rasping, "Lick them, eat them, fill me, stretch me."

The words ignited Ed's thick large member as it impaled her wet captivated pleasure, ravaging in its stretching as it penetrated deeper into her tunnel.

Kayra gripped his organ as she rode and ground him into her.

She came rapidly as fingernails dug deep into his smooth hairless back, screaming feverishly as her core filled in, accepting the prize of hot gushing semen.

Her grinding and moaning slowed as his load waned.

Ed gasped and exhaled adding warm air to the steamed-up windscreen as her grip slowly released his cock. Kayra's nails gently stroked his spine following the trail of blood from her passionate grip. She disentangled herself from Ed's expended cock, sliding over onto the driver's seat, offering him a post-coital cigarette. He accepted it happily, drawing hard after lighting, filling his lungs with smoke as his body filled with nicotine. Kayra wiggled back into her tight faux-leather trousers as she smoked, not bothering to add her bra or knickers.

"What now? I'm still game." Ed was aware that his penis was still erect and able to perform. Her earlier proposal helped foster the urge for more.

Kayra was happy with his words, as she too wanted further sex, and besides that, her intention of a threesome would increase her points within the group. The thought of Ed's cock being jointly shared with another kept her already-stretched vagina wet in fevered anticipation.

"That was my pact - if you gave me a good seeing to. Are you sure you want to share Mr. Bulge with two mouths and two pussies?"

"Why not. What man in his right mind could say no?"

"True," said Kayra. "I bet you can get us both to come with your huge cock."

Ed had never fucked two women in the same place before, and at his age if he did not take the offered opportunity, he might regret it on his deathbed. He was still not sure if she was teasing him and did not expect an actual threesome, but her words drove his desire (or it could have been the Viagra) to at least fuck Kayra again.

"What the hell," he thought, "you only live once."

On the journey to her small, bought council flat, the pair examined the word "fuckbuddy" and agreed that while both single, "why not?" as long as they were both comfortable in the arrangement. Ed persuaded her that occasionally he needed a date for business events, which she agreed to provide if he reciprocated. By the time they arrived at her place she felt their arrangement was a good thing and decided days or evenings out without sex may be worth a try. Once past his shyness, Ed was an okay bloke.

The journey took twenty-five minutes, during which they held hands as if full-time lovers, expanding their chat into other areas.

Kayra parked the VW in its designated spot. After switching the car's engine off, she made a suggestion.

"Wanna see what you look like as you fuck?"

Ed had forgotten about the car's security camera as she pressed a sequence of buttons on the dashcam and picked up her smartphone from the car's centre console, scrolled down to a compatible app and pressed play.

It was clear – an in-focus film of pure, unedited

fucking. Kayra wanted to make sure her man-mountain was ready for more. She was surprised at how vocal she was at the moment of climax. Ed viewed intently.

“I'll Whatsapp you a copy if you like.” She sent it to him before he answered.

They smooched passionately before stepping out of her car.

“I’m on the third floor - no lift, I'm afraid. Well, there is, but it has been broken for months.”

As they walked up the block stairwell, Kayra sent a text.

Ed, a few steps back, his nostrils full of the distinct smell of urine, was crushing spent needles underfoot. He began focusing on Kayra’s posterior as it moved with her physique in a full seductive deliberate motion. Kayra pushed a scuffed white fire door which led to her floor, a small open-air corridor with a concrete floor, littered with cigarette butts and general rubbish. The front doors of the flats were all the same and freshly painted red. The one redeeming feature was the view from the outside lobby. Looking across the balcony you could see the shiny modern glass buildings of London’s Square Mile, and to the right, the green of Essex pasture.

Kayra stopped outside red door number 33, distinct in design from the others with its gold door number, matching knocker, and letterbox.

Kayra’s keys, already in hand, unlocked the door

with Ed not noticing that she only unlocked one of the two locks.

On opening she walked in, Ed following. He shut the door not having an opportunity to take in the surroundings as she threw her arms around him, kissing him as if he were a long-lost lover, not one of carnal knowledge an hour earlier.

“My manners! Where's my hospitality to a guest?” she said breaking off from their warm embrace.

Kayra opened one of the doors off the small hallway.

“The living room - it's not much but it's mine. Take a seat. What would you like to drink?”

“A beer if you have one, please.”

Ed sat down on the comfy looking but worn sofa, noticing the side table with a lipstick smudged tumbler half-filled with whisky and an uncapped Jack Daniel’s bottle beside it. A large TV screen attached to the wall was on standby mode.

He heard Kayra open what he assumed was the fridge door, along with other sounds of clutter. She soon emerged holding a cold bottled beer and an empty glass.

Handing him his bottle, she said, “Can you pour me one while I use the bathroom? I will be two minutes.”

Ed sat back on the three-seater sofa, taking a long swig from the cold bottle. He was sure he could hear muffled laughter coming from somewhere in the apartment as he poured a double Jack Daniel’s. Kayra reappeared in a silky red baby-doll set and not much else, glancing at Ed as she picked up and gulped down the contents of the glass, pouring herself another into the lipstick-stained glass.

She handed Ed the lipstick-free glass.

"Cheers Ed, how fuckable am I in this?"

She bent forward, giving Ed an eyeful of her cleavage, clinking his glass as she sat down beside him.

Ed was still sure he heard movement from elsewhere in the flat but ignored it and responded by spontaneously kissing her full lips, tasting freshly added lip-gloss. She responded in reaching between his legs finding his stiffness, moaning in pleasure as her eager mouth engaged with his whilst Ed's hand was finding and squeezing her breasts over the silky lingerie. Kayra continued to moan as Ed gently pinched a nipple before running his hands down past her navel ring, paying homage between her rich smooth thighs, her bud opening to worshipping fingers, fulfilling their quest of glorious exploration.

Kayra's body quivered as fingers discovered her G-Spot, climaxing over its stimulation, gasping in pure unadulterated ecstasy.

"Wow! It's been... I don't know how long since a man could find it, I had given up hope of a man's fingers hitting my spot. Usually, I rely on self-stimulation."

"A man should always know how to fulfil a woman's

pleasure."

"Err not sure how I should say this," she continued, "but with your size and finger expertise, have you have thought about the porn industry? Girls wouldn't need to falsify for the camera."

Ed confessed she was not the first to propose a dirty picture career.

"My age is against me."

"Working nearly nine inches with your physique is ageless. Perhaps additional practice," she said, looking seriously at him.

"Thanks for the compliment," he said emptying the tumbler, pouring two more. Ed, again, was sure he heard something. He could not pinpoint it, whatever the whirring sound was - but he was positive that he was right.

He was right in his hypothesis, for on the queen-size bed in the next room, Kayra's police friend, Lisa, was warming herself up with a seven-inch vibrator. It was actually her who proposed a three-way shag after meeting Kayra at the earlier police stop. Kayra's job was to keep schtum but suggest his worthiness in porno as a way around recording the event for the group to watch, score and of course later enjoy. In their view, porn was not only for the males of this world.

Lisa, clad in her police uniform without bra or knickers, breasts tight against her white police shirt had set the scene: police-issue handcuffs with one end attached to the bed frame, waiting for their captive, complete with scented massage oils, and candles - the dripping kind - ready to tease. She had even learnt a basic script.

In the first scene, Lisa was to remain invisible, filming with her smartphone. As Kayra, about to go down on Ed's massive cock, shouts "Help, help! Large cock at large, I need assistance to arrest it and hold it in my mouth, come quick!"

Cheesy, deliberately, but are most pornos not like this?

"Additional practice." Kayra repeated herself, looking deep into Ed's eyes as she came down from her orgasm.

Ed understood she was not kidding and wanted to film their sexual action. Kayra intended to offer more head: eight inches stretching her mouth could become an addiction.

Ed's cock was fully immersed as she stood up, legs apart, fingers opening her essence, sparkling in intoxicating, succulent after-cum.

Her hand reached for his as she led him to her bedroom and its hidden reality.

Rachel Comes Again...

Rachel did indeed powder her nose, and on retrieving her lip-gloss she found a small forgotten package of cocaine, given to her by a trusted friend months ago. The friend suggested it increased libido. Rachel decided tonight was the night to relax. Nervously emptying the small package onto the edge of the white, sparkling-clean washbasin, she cut two non-straight lines and, without thinking, snorted the substance through one nostril. The drug was absorbed by her brain in seconds. Sniffing hard, wiping the residue from under her nose before adding gloss to her lips, she started looking into the wide wall mirror behind the washbasin.

Staring into the mirror, admiring her image, she retrieved her mobile and composed a sext message to her hot date.

"Come find me, I'm waiting for you to take me from behind."

Rachel was aware she only had a few minutes until Josh found her. Her text to him was left unanswered. Staring at the blank screen, waiting for his words, her mind intent on wants and desire, she wanted a first date fucking here, right now in a public restroom. The dating game fully immersed her thoughts alone in the room, waiting for her handsome "Pick Up". Her hand slipped under her black skirt, finding the heart of unhindered femininity. Her mound was damp from the evening's pent-up exhilaration. A finger eased easily into her vibrant moisture. Rachel admired her vertical nipples, hard with pending excitement. Her free hand undid another button on her blouse, revealing a blue figure-hugging bra. Pinching one nipple with her thumb and forefinger, she began immediately sending excess ripples of lust to her slit.

Her heart pounded in ecstasy, beating within her desire as her ears listened intently. The restroom door opened; she hoped it was the pickup. Eyes shut tight, approaching footsteps engulfed her ears, pussy lips desperate for her date's fingers. The footsteps stopped, warm breath directly behind her, all five senses alert to movement. Two strong arms from behind wrapped themselves around her breasts, hands cupping and squeezing. Her head turned, eyes closed, mouth open, eager for another's lips. Rachel felt a mouth nibble her upper lip. Tasting and feeling a whisky-laden tongue, it discovers hers, a hand was frantically working its way down her body, slipping within her skirt, finding her hand and wetness.

The mouth was kissing harder and deeper, creating a fervent need in Rachel's arousal, a hardness pushing on her back. Her mouth was sucking and engulfing his tongue. She turned forward, parting their locked mouths, bending forward over the basin. Her hand gripped, waiting for what was to enter from behind. Hearing him unbuckle, her eyes remained closed. Hot strong bare legs forced hers apart.

Her panting was urging him on.

One hand forced her body further forward, clenching the basin harder, as another hand pulled her skirt up, exposing her entrance, folds wet with longing, prying fingers giving way to a thick, rough cock, entering, ramming deep, penetrating.

"Be rough," she screamed. "Fuck me like never before!"

The hand pushed her head further into the basin, pulling her hair tight as the Pick-Up's thrust ravaged her needy pussy. Rachels's face was hit by droplets of water as her hand grabbed the pushdown tap. Her clit was throbbing at the cock's rough hard invasion, devouring slamming thrusts. Rachel could not help the loud groans, which made him trust harder, banging against her bare arse.

A strong hand, controlling her thrusting thighs, slapped her exposed arse intermittently, the other pushing the middle of her back. He plunged in and out of her pulsating pussy. Her head in the basin was wet with a mixture of sweat and water. She clenched the tap waiting for *that* moment.

Rachel's fanny consumed the cock as it ejaculated its warm juice deep inside her. She screamed into the basin as it filled her, detonating her own orgasm of desire, finding her inner nymphomania.

She peered up into the mirror, squinting. She was sure a distant face was looking back at her.

It was not Josh, the face looking grainy and almost unreal. The other face, too, was male. Her clouded mind told her it was the handsome stranger who had hit on her earlier. Rachel was sure Josh had not seen the voyeur. The face's eyes locked with hers intently.

Her pussy muscles reaffirmed their grip on the cock inside her, spent, but still hard. Rachel stared into the mirror looking at Josh's odd image. She stammered and spoke to the mirror. The cock pulled out of her vagina as she spoke and stood upright, both her hands resting on the mirror. The face pulled back into the shadows of the room, leaving its hormonal scent to linger. Rachel spoke to Josh's non-moving image without turning around. She too stood straight, pulling up her skirt slowly for the pleasure of the hidden face. Her eyes again closed, mouthing her question to Josh.

"Is tonight still up to me? Can I keep exploring my boundaries?"

"It's your night, it's for whatever you desire."

Rachel mouthed at the mirror "Can I fuck a real stranger while you watch?"

She looked into the mirror. Words were not spoken back to her. Rachel was sure the stranger stepped out from its shadow. Her eyes closed again, feeling the dull thud of footsteps on the room's surface. The footsteps suggested a large man. Grunting sounds suggested he was wanking.

As the grunting sounds grew louder, she bent down slowly, snorting the remainder of the white powder. Rachel knew she wanted the stranger's cock inside her. Her fingers were inside, wet with her cum, wishing to experience another man's penis. Josh did not respond to her.

Rachel craved more, her legs still apart, fingering under her skirt, needing to get off again. The answer was required to help her cum.

She heard a whisper in her ear.

"Yeah, go fuck another man if you want to; we did agree whatever you wanna do - but only tonight."

Rachel squinted at the mirror, its haze harder to comprehend as the drug fuelled her fresh desire. A man stepped forward holding a large stiff cock.

A thought struck her: the image in the mirror must-have watched them screw.

Frantically, fingers stroked her clit. Her mind told her Josh was watching as the man approached her.

"Go ahead, fuck her hard while I watch."

Her fingers pushed deeper inside, her entire body quivered as she finally climaxed.

Rachel, spent, turned around; Josh and the stranger were not there. She gazed back at the mirror and saw only her face starring back at her.

Her cocaine-induced trance confused her brain as she came down, slowly, back to reality.

Rachel was no longer in the ladies.

Catching her breath, she asked, "Was there another man here, or are we just high?"

"Err no, Rachel, no other person. I'm not high, just perhaps a bit drunk. We were at the bar, you said you needed to powder your nose - but that was thirty minutes ago."

Rachel looked at Josh, feeling like she had orgasmed. Between her legs was warm and sticky.

It dawned on her that, somehow, she had actually orgasmed. Her mind was blank.

"What happened Josh, tell me?"

"I don't know. I've been sat here for twenty minutes and ordered you a fillet steak with fries."

Rachel was totally confused.

"Did I send you a text?"

Josh handed her his smartphone, showing no new text messages. She checked her smartphone for sent messages. There were none, not since yesterday, but she did find a not-sent text:

"Come find me, I'm waiting for you to take me from behind."

The facts hit her after discretely feeling between her legs. It was moist and sore from excessive touching.

"Everything okay, Rachel?"

"Yes, darling. I'm feeling a bit hot and lightheaded," she said, realising what had happened earlier. Was it just her imagination that had got her off, or did a real stranger actually fuck her? Rachel was not 100% sure, especially as at that moment the handsome stranger who had hit on her at the bar walked past their table, winking salaciously at Rachel.

However, she was desperate, and sure she wanted her husband's cock to deeply penetrate her.

The End...

About the Publisher

L.R. Price Publications is dedicated to publishing books by unknown authors. We use a mixture of both traditional and modern publishing options, to bring our authors' words to the wider world. We print, publish, distribute and market books in a variety of formats including paper and hardback, electronic books, digital audiobooks and online.

If you are an author interested in getting your book published, or a book retailer interested in selling our books, please contact us.

www.lrpricepublications.com

L.R. Price Publications Ltd,

27 Old Gloucester Street,

London, WC1N 3AX.

020 3051 9572

Email: publishing@lrprice.com

Printed in Great Britain
by Amazon

45985285R00178